Please return/renew this item by the
last date shown to avoid a charge.
Books may also be renewed by phone
and Internet. May not be renewed if
required by another reader.

www.libraries.barnet.gov.uk

BARNET
LONDON BOROUGH

Maria Semple spent fifteen years in Los Angeles as a television writer, working on hit shows including *Ellen*, *Saturday Night Live*, *Mad About You* and *Arrested Development*. Her second novel, *Where'd You Go, Bernadette,* was shortlisted for the 2013 Women's Prize for Fiction and won the 2013 Melissa Nathan Award. Maria lives in Seattle.

www.mariasemple.com

Also by Maria Semple

Where'd You Go, Bernadette
This One Is Mine

Praise for Today Will Be Different

'Whip-smart, dazzling, darkly comic and deeply touching. I loved it!'   Marian Keyes, author of *The Woman Who Stole My Life*

'A dark, pop-culture-stuffed take on *Mrs Dalloway* that sees Semple once again writing about a difficult woman with gleeful empathy and humour that can turn on a knife edge to heartbreak'   *Red*

'I love Maria Semple. *Today Will Be Different* is just as funny, poignant, and life-affirming as *Bernadette*'

Nina Stibbe, author of *Love, Nina* and *Man at the Helm*

'Coolly comic, sharply observant . . . This whip-smart, bleakly humorous study of how we live now is full of finely drawn characters and deserves to widen [Semple's] fanbase'   *Sunday Times*

'Semple reaffirms her gift for creating memorable, monstrous characters . . . Semple is skilled in holding back revelations and planting clues to later emotional payoffs. Somehow she makes her seethingly intolerant and dissatisfied heroines lovable for all their flaws'   *Guardian*

'Captivating, right up to the final twist'   *Grazia*

'So unique, so smart, so funny, so beautifully humane, so utterly of our times, it's astonishing'   Gillian Flynn, author of *Gone Girl*

'Neurotic, scatty and fretting about her marriage, son, career and endless #firstworldproblems, Eleanor Flood would be a nightmare friend – but as a comic creation, she's a dream . . . With its sparky gags and quirky cast of characters, never has a meltdown been so entertaining'   *Glamour*

'Smart, funny and original'   *Good Housekeeping*

Praise for *Where'd You Go, Bernadette*

**Shortlisted for the 2013 Women's Prize for Fiction
and winner of the 2013 Melissa Nathan Award**

'Fresh and funny and accomplished, but the best thing about it was that I never had any idea what was going to happen next. It was a wild ride'   Kate Atkinson

'An invigorating, hilarious, addictive ride of a novel'
                                                    Maggie O'Farrell

'Semple's epistolary novel satirizes Seattle, Microsoft, helicopter parents, the elite, and the overeducated – while revealing truths about family, genius, ambition, and resilience'   Gillian Flynn

'I have hardly stopped raving about this since I read it . . . Funny, poignant and pointed, think Jennifer Egan's *Goon Squad* rewritten by Tina Fey and you get the picture. Without doubt, my book of the year'   Sam Baker, *Red*

'The characters in *Bernadette* may be in real emotional pain, but Semple has the wit and perspective and imagination to make their story hilarious. I tore through this book with heedless pleasure'   Jonathan Franzen

'Maria Semple dissects the gory complexities of familial dysfunction with a deft and tender hand. *Where'd You Go, Bernadette* is a triumph of social observation and black comedy by a skilful chronicler of moneyed malaise'   Patrick deWitt

'As sharp as lemon juice'   Wendy Holden, *Daily Mail*

'[A] heart-warming, life-affirming novel of the year'   *The Times*

TODAY WILL BE DIFFERENT

MARIA SEMPLE

WEIDENFELD & NICOLSON

A W&N PAPERBACK

First published in Great Britain in 2016 by Weidenfeld & Nicolson
This paperback edition published in 2017 by Weidenfeld & Nicolson
an imprint of the Orion Publishing Group Ltd
Carmelite House, 50 Victoria Embankment
London EC4Y 0DZ

An Hachette UK Company

1 3 5 7 9 10 8 6 4 2

A CIP catalogue record for this book is
available from the British Library.

ISBN (mass market paperback) 978 1 78022 733 7
ISBN (eBook) 978 0 297 87147 7

Printed in Great Britain by CPI Group (UK) Ltd, Croydon, CR0 4YY

www.orionbooks.co.uk

For George and Poppy
and, to a lesser extent, Ralphy

Today will be different. Today I will be present. Today, anyone I speak to, I will look them in the eye and listen deeply. Today I'll play a board game with Timby. I'll initiate sex with Joe. Today I will take pride in my appearance. I'll shower, get dressed in proper clothes, and change into yoga clothes only for yoga, which today I will actually attend. Today I won't swear. I won't talk about money. Today there will be an ease about me. My face will be relaxed, its resting place a smile. Today I will radiate calm. Kindness and self-control will abound. Today I will buy local. Today I will be my best self, the person I'm capable of being. Today will be different.

The Trick

Because the other way wasn't working. The waking up just to get the day over with until it was time for bed. The grinding it out was a disgrace, an affront to the honor and long shot of being alive at all. The ghost-walking, the short-tempered distraction, the hurried fog. (All of this I'm just assuming, because I have no idea how I come across, my consciousness is that underground, like a toad in winter.) The leaving the world a worse place just by being in it. The blindness to the destruction in my wake. The Mr. Magoo.

If I'm forced to be honest, here's an account of how I left the world last week: worse, worse, better, worse, same, worse, same. Not an inventory to make one swell with pride. I don't necessarily need to make the world a better place, mind you. Today, I will live by the Hippocratic oath: first do no harm.

How hard can it be? Dropping off Timby, having my poetry lesson (my favorite part of life!), taking a yoga class, eating lunch with Sydney Madsen, whom I can't stand but at least I can check her off the list (more on that later), picking up Timby, and giving back to Joe, the underwriter of all this mad abundance.

You're trying to figure out, why the *agita* surrounding one normal day of white-people problems? Because there's me and there's the beast in me. It would be kind of brilliant if the beast in me played out on a giant canvas, shocking and awe-ing, causing fabulous destruction, talked about forever. If I could swing that, I just might:

self-immolate gloriously for the performance-art spectacle. The sad truth? The beast in me plays out on a painfully small scale: regrettable micro-transactions usually involving Timby, my friends, or Joe. I'm irritable and consumed by anxiety when I'm with them; maudlin and shit-talking when I'm not. Ha! Aren't you glad you're at a safe distance, doors locked, windows rolled up? Aw, come on. I'm nice. I'm exaggerating for effect. It's not really like that.

And so the day began, the minute I whipped off my sheets. The *click-click-click* of Yo-Yo's nails across the hardwood, stopping outside the bedroom. Why, when Joe whips off his sheets, doesn't Yo-Yo *trot-trot-trot* and wait in abject hope? How can Yo-Yo, on the other side of a closed door, tell it's me and not Joe? It was once depressingly explained by a dog trainer: it's my smell Yo-Yo's caught whiff of. That his idea of nirvana is a dead seal washed up on the beach leaves me asking, Is it time for bed yet? Nope, I'm not doing that. Not today.

I didn't mean to be coy about Sydney Madsen.

When Joe and I arrived in Seattle from New York ten years ago, we were ready to start a family. I'd just wrapped five wearying years at *Looper Wash*. Everywhere you looked it was *Looper Wash* T-shirts, bumper stickers, mouse pads. *I'm a Vivian. I'm a Dot.* You remember. If not, check your nearest dollar store, the two-for-one bin, it's been a while.

Joe, a hand surgeon, had become a legend of sorts for reconstructing the hand of that quarterback whose thumb bent back and nobody thought he'd ever play again but the next year he went on to win the Super Bowl. (I can't remember his name, but even if I did, I couldn't say, due to doctor/patient/nosy-wife confidentiality.)

Joe had job offers everywhere. Why pick Seattle? Joe, a nice Catholic boy from outside Buffalo, couldn't see raising kids in Manhattan, my first choice. We struck a deal. We'd move anywhere he wanted for ten years, and back to New York for ten; his city for ten, my city for ten, back and forth, unto death. (A deal he's conveniently forgotten his end of, I might add, seeing as we're coming up on year ten and not a peep on packing up.)

As everybody knows, being raised Catholic with half a brain means becoming an atheist. At one of our skeptics' conventions (yes, our early years were actually spent doing things like driving to Philadelphia to watch Penn Jillette debate a rabbi! Oh, to be childless again... or not), Joe heard that Seattle was the least religious city in America. Seattle it was.

A Doctors Without Borders board member threw Joe and me a welcome-to-town party. I swanned into her Lake Washington mansion filled with modern art and future friends, mine for the taking. My whole life, I've been liked. Okay, I'll say it: I've been adored. I don't understand why, on account of my disgraceful personality, but somehow it works. Joe says it's because I'm the most guy-like woman he's ever met, but sexy and with no emotional membrane. (A compliment!) I went from room to room, being introduced to a series of women, interchangeable in their decency and warmth. It was that thing where you meet somebody who tells you they like camping and you say, "Oh! I was just talking to someone who's going on a ten-day rafting trip down the Snake River, you should totally meet them," and the person says, "That was me."

What can I say? I'm terrible with faces. And names. And numbers. And times. And dates.

The whole party was a blur, with one woman eager to show me funky shops, another hidden hikes, another Mario Batali's father's Italian restaurant in Pioneer Square, another the best dentist in town who has a glitter painting on his ceiling of a parachuting tiger, yet another willing to share her housekeeper. One of them, Sydney Madsen, invited me to lunch the next day at the Tamarind Tree in the International District.

(Joe has a thing he calls the magazine test. It's the reaction you have when you open the mailbox and pull out a magazine. Instantly, you know if you're happy to see this magazine or bummed. Which is why I don't subscribe to *The New Yorker* and do subscribe to *Us Weekly*. Put to the magazine test, Sydney Madsen is the human equivalent of *Tinnitus Today*.)

That first lunch: She was so careful with her words, so sincere in her gaze, noticed a small spot on her fork and was overly solicitous toward the waiter when asking for a new one, brought her own tea bag and asked for hot water, said she wasn't very hungry so how about we split my green papaya salad, told me she'd never seen *Looper Wash* but would put a hold on the DVDs at the library.

Am I painting a clear enough picture of the tight-assed dreariness, the selfish cluelessness, the cheap creepiness? A water-stained fork never killed anybody! *Buy* the DVDs, how about? Eat the food at the restaurant, that's how they stay in business! Worst of all, Sydney Madsen was steady, earnest, without a speck of humor, and talked… very… slowly… as… if… her… platitudes… were… little… gold… coins.

I was in shock. Living too long in New York does that to a girl, gives her the false sense that the world is full of interesting people. Or at least people who are crazy in an interesting way.

At one point I writhed so violently in my chair that Sydney actually asked, "Do you need to use the powder room?" (Powder room? *Powder room?* Kill her!) The worst part? All those women with whom I'd gladly agreed to go hiking and shopping? They weren't a bunch of women. They were all Sydney Madsen! Damn that blur! It took everything I had to kink her fire hose of new invitations: a weekend at her beach house on Vashon Island, introducing me to the wife of someone for this, the playwright of something for that.

I ran home screaming to Joe.

Joe: You should have been suspicious of someone so eager to make friends, because it probably means she doesn't have any.

Me: This is why I love you, Joe. You just boil it all down. (Joe the boiler. Don't we just love him?)

Forgive me for long-hauling you on Sydney Madsen. My point is: for ten years I haven't been able to shake her. She's the friend I don't like, the friend I don't know what she does for a living because I was too stultified to ask the first time and it would be rude to ask now (because I'm not rude), the friend I can't be mean enough to so she gets the message (because I'm not mean), the friend to whom I keep saying no, no, no, yet she still chases me. She's like Parkinson's, you can't cure her, you can just manage the symptoms.

For today, the lunch bell tolls.

Please know I'm aware that lunch with a boring person *is* a boutique problem. When I say I have problems, I'm not talking about Sydney Madsen.

Yo-Yo trotting down the street, the prince of Belltown. Oh, Yo-Yo, you foolish creature with your pep and your blind devotion and your busted ear flapping with every prance. How poignant it is, the pride you take in being walked by me, your immortal beloved. If only you knew.

What a disheartening spectacle it's been, a new month, a new condo higher than the last, each packed with blue-badged Amazon squids, every morning squirting by the thousands from their studio apartments onto my block, heads in devices, never looking up. (They work for Amazon, so you know they're soulless. The only question, how soulless?) It makes me pine for the days when Third Ave. was just me, empty storefronts and the one tweaker yelling, "*That's* how you spell America!"

Outside our building, Dennis stood by his wheelie trash can and refilled the poop-bag dispenser. "Good morning, you two."

"Good morning, Dennis!" Instead of my usual breezing past, I stopped and looked him in the eye. "How's your day so far?"

"Oh, can't complain," he said. "You?"

"Can complain, but won't."

Dennis chuckled.

Today, already a net gain.

I opened the front door of our apartment. At the end of the hallway: Joe face down at the table, his forehead flat on the newspaper, arms splayed with bent elbows as if under arrest.

It was a jarring image, one of pure defeat, the last thing I'd ever associate with Joe —

Thunk.

The door shut. I unclipped Yo-Yo's harness. By the time I straightened, my stricken husband had gotten up and disappeared into his office. Whatever it was, he didn't want to talk about it.

My attitude? Works for me!

Yo-Yo raced to his food, greyhound-style, back legs vaulting past his front. Realizing it was the same dry food that had been there before his walk, he became overwhelmed with confusion and betrayal. He took one step and stared at a spot on the floor.

Timby's light clicked on. God bless him, up before the alarm. I went into his bathroom and found him on the step stool in his PJs.

"Morning, darling. Look at you, up and awake."

He stopped what he was doing. "Can we have bacon?"

Timby, in the mirror, waited for me to leave. I lowered my eyes. The little Quick Draw McGraw beat my glance. He pushed something into the sink before I could see it. The unmistakable clang of lightweight plastic. The Sephora 200!

It was nobody's fault but my own, Santa putting a makeup kit in Timby's stocking. It's how I'd buy myself extra time at Nordstrom, telling Timby to roam cosmetics. The girls there loved his gentle nature, his sugar-sack body, his squeaky voice. Soon enough, they were making him up. I don't know if he liked the makeup as much as being doted on by a gaggle of blondes. On a lark, I picked up a kit the size of a paperback that unfolded and fanned out to reveal six different makeup trays (!) holding two hundred (!) shadows, glosses, blushes, and whatever-they-weres. The person who'd found a way to cram so much into so little should seriously be working for NASA. If they still have that.

"You do realize you're not wearing makeup to school," I told him.

"I know, Mom." The sigh and shoulder heave right out of the Disney Channel. Again, my bad for letting it take root. After school, a jigsaw puzzle!

I emerged from Timby's room. Yo-Yo, standing anxiously,

shivered with relief upon seeing that I still existed. Knowing I'd be heading to the kitchen to make breakfast, he raced me to his food bowl. This time he deigned to eat some, one eye on me.

Joe was back and making himself tea.

"How's things?" I asked.

"Don't you look nice," he said.

True to my grand scheme for the day, I'd showered and put on a dress and oxfords. If you beheld my closet, you'd see a woman of specific style. Dresses from France and Belgium, price tags ripped off before I got home because Joe would have an aneurysm, and every iteration of flat black shoe . . . again, no need to discuss price. Buy them? Yes. Put them on? On most days, too much energy.

"Olivia's coming tonight," I said with a wink, already tasting the wine flight and rigatoni at Tavolàta.

"How about she takes Timby out so we can have a little alone time?" Joe grabbed me by the waist and pulled me in as if we weren't a couple of fifty-year-olds.

Here's who I envy: lesbians. Why? Lesbian bed death. Apparently, after a lesbian couple's initial flush of hot sex, they stop having it altogether. It makes perfect sense. Left to their own devices, women would stop having sex after they have children. There's no evolutionary need for it. Our brains know it, our body knows it. Who feels sexy during the slog of motherhood, the middle-aged fat roll and the flattening butt? What woman wants anyone to see her naked, let alone fondle her breasts, squishy now like bags of cake batter, or touch her stomach, spongy like breadfruit? Who wants to pretend they're all sexed up when the honeypot is dry?

Me, that's who, if I don't want to get switched out for a younger model.

"Alone time it is," I said to Joe.

"Mom, this broke." Timby came in with his ukulele and plonked it down on the counter. Suspiciously near the trash. "The sound's all messed up."

"What do you propose we do?" I asked, daring him to say, *Buy a new one.*

Joe picked up the ukulele and strummed. "It's a little out of tune, that's all." He began to adjust the strings.

"Hey," I said. "Since when can you tune a ukulele?"

"I'm a man of many mysteries," Joe said and gave the instrument a final dulcet strum.

The bacon and French toast were being wolfed, the smoothies being drunk. Timby was deep into an *Archie Double Digest*. My smile was on lockdown.

Two years ago when I was getting all martyr-y about having to make breakfast every morning, Joe said, "I pay for this circus. Can you please climb down off your cross and make breakfast without the constant sighing?"

I know what you're going to say: *What a jerk! What a sexist thug!* But Joe had a point. Lots of women would gladly do worse for a closet full of Antwerp. From that moment on, it was service with a smile. It's called knowing when you've got a weak hand.

Joe showed Timby the newspaper. "The Pinball Expo is coming back to town. Wanna go?"

"Do you think the Evel Knievel machine will still be broken?"

"Almost certainly," Joe said.

I handed over the poem I'd printed out and heavily annotated.

"Okay, who's going to help me?" I asked.

Timby didn't look up from his *Archie*.

Joe took it. "Ooh, Robert Lowell."

Skunk Hour

[handwritten note in cloud: 8:30 Thursday Lola, Oct. 8th]

By Robert Lowell

(For Elizabeth Bishop)

Nautilus Island's hermit
heiress still lives through winter in her Spartan cottage;
her sheep still graze above the sea.
Her son's a bishop. Her farmer
is first selectman in our village;
she's in her dotage.

[handwritten: showing or characterized by austerity — Ancient Sparta]

[handwritten: HER]

Thirsting for
the hierarchic privacy
of Queen Victoria's century,
she buys up all
the eyesores facing her shore,
and lets them fall.

[handwritten: impressions of a sea village after summer — heading into winter]

The season's ill—
we've lost our summer millionaire,
who seemed to leap from an L. L. Bean
catalogue. His nine-knot yawl
was auctioned off to lobstermen.
A red fox stain covers Blue Hill.

[handwritten: OUR]

And now our fairy
decorator brightens his shop for fall;
his fishnet's filled with orange cork,
orange, his cobbler's bench and awl;
there is no money in his work,
he'd rather marry.

[handwritten: tool for piercing holes in leather]

16

One dark night,
my Tudor Ford climbed the hill's skull;
I watched for love-cars. Lights turned down,
they lay together, hull to hull,
where the graveyard shelves on the town. . . .
My mind's not right.

A car radio bleats,
"Love, O careless Love. . . ." I hear
my ill-spirit sob in each blood cell,
as if my hand were at its throat. . . .
I myself am hell;
nobody's here—

only skunks, that search
in the moonlight for a bite to eat.
They march on their soles up Main Street:
white stripes, moonstruck eyes' red fire
under the chalk dry and spar spire
of the Trinitarian Church.

I stand on top
of our back steps and breathe the rich air—
a mother skunk with her column of kittens swills the garbage pail
She jabs her wedge-head in a cup
of sour cream, drops her ostrich tail,
and will not scare.

I began from memory: "'Nautical Island's hermit heiress still lives through winter in her Spartan cottage; her sheep still graze above the sea. Her son's a bishop. Her farmer's first selectman'—"

"'Her farmer *is* first selectman,'" Joe said.

"Shoot. 'Her farmer *is* first selectman.'"

"Mom!"

I shushed Timby and continued with eyes closed. "'...in our village; she's in her dotage. Thirsting for the hierarchic privacy of Queen Victoria's century, she buys up all the eyesores facing her shore, and lets them fall. The season's ill—we've lost our summer millionaire, who seemed to leap from an L. L. Bean catalogue'—"

"Mommy, look at Yo-Yo. See how his chin is sitting on his paws?"

Yo-Yo was positioned on his pink lozenge so he could watch for dropped food, his little white paws delicately crossed.

"Aww," I said.

"Can I have your phone?" Timby asked.

"Just enjoy your pet," I said. "This doesn't have to turn into electronics."

"It's very cool what Mom is doing," Joe said to Timby. "Always learning."

"Learning and forgetting," I said. "But thank you."

He shot me an air kiss.

I pressed onward. "'His nine-knot yawl was auctioned off to lobstermen'—"

"Don't we love Yo-Yo?" Timby asked.

"We do." The simple truth. Yo-Yo is the world's cutest dog, part Boston terrier, part pug, part something else...brindle-and-white with a black patch on one eye, bat ears, smooshed face, and curlicue tail. Before the Amazon invasion, when it was just me and hookers on the street, one remarked, "It's like if Barbie had a pit bull."

"Daddy," Timby said. "Don't you love Yo-Yo?"

Joe looked at Yo-Yo and considered the question. (More evidence of Joe's superiority: he thinks before he speaks.)

"He's a little weird," Joe said and returned to the poem.

Timby dropped his fork. I dropped my jaw.

"*Weird?*" Timby cried.

Joe looked up. "Yeah. What?"

"Oh, Daddy! How can you say that?"

"He just sits there all day looking depressed," Joe said. "When we come home, he doesn't greet us at the door. When we are here, he just sleeps, waits for food to drop, or stares at the front door like he has a migraine."

For Timby and me, there were simply no words.

"I know what he's getting out of *us,*" Joe said. "I just don't know what we're getting out of *him.*"

Timby jumped out of his chair and lay across Yo-Yo, his version of a hug. "Oh, Yo-Yo! *I* love you."

"Keep going." Joe flicked the poem. "You're doing great. 'The season's ill' …"

" 'The season's ill,' " I said. " 'We've lost our summer millionaire, who seemed to leap from an L. L. Bean catalogue' —" To Timby: "You. Get ready."

"Are we driving through or are you walking me in?"

"Driving. I have Alonzo at eight thirty."

Our breakfast over, Yo-Yo got up from his pillow. Joe and I watched as he walked to the front door and stared at it.

"I didn't realize I was being controversial," Joe said. " 'The season's ill.' "

It's easy to tell who went to Catholic school by how they react when they drive up Queen Anne Hill and behold the Galer Street School. I didn't, so to me it's a stately brick building with a huge flat yard and improbably dynamite view of the Puget Sound. Joe did, so he goes white with flashbacks of nuns whacking his hands with rulers, priests threatening him with God's wrath, and spectacle-snatching bullies roaming the halls unchecked.

By the time we pulled into drop-off, I'd recited the poem twice perfectly and was doing it a third time for charm. "'One dark night, my Tudor Ford climbed the hill's skull.' Wait, is that right?"

Ominous silence from the backseat. "Hey," I said. "Are you even following along?"

"I am, Mom. You're doing perfect."

"*Perfectly*. Adverbs end in *l-y*." Timby wasn't in the rearview mirror. I figure-eighted it to see him hunched over something. "What are you doing?"

"Nothing." Followed again by that high-pitched rattle of plastic.

"Hey! No makeup."

"Then why did Santa put it in my stocking?"

I turned around but Timby's door had opened and shut. By the time I swung back, he was bounding up the front steps. In the reflection of the school's front door, I caught Timby's eyelids smeared with rouge. I rolled down my window.

"You little sneak, get back here!"

The car behind me honked. Ah, well, he was the school's problem now.

Me peeling out of Galer Street with seven child-free hours on the horizon? Cue the banjo getaway music.

" 'I myself am hell; nobody's here — only skunks, that search in the moonlight for a bite to eat. They march on their soles up Main Street: white stripes, moonstruck eyes' red fire under the chalk-dry and spar spire of the Trinitarian Church. I stand on top of our back steps and breathe the rich air — a mother skunk with her column of kittens swills the garbage pail. She jabs her wedge-head in a cup of sour cream, drops her ostrich tail, and will not scare.' "

I'd nailed it, syllable for syllable.

Alonzo stuck out his hand. "Congratulations."

You know how your brain turns to mush? How it starts when you're pregnant? You laugh, full of wonder and conspiracy, and you chide yourself, Me and my pregnancy brain! Then you give birth and your brain doesn't return? But you're breast-feeding, so you laugh, as if you're a member of an exclusive club? *Me and my nursing brain!* But then you stop nursing and the terrible truth descends: Your good brain is never coming back. You've traded vocabulary, lucidity, and memory for motherhood. You know how you're in the middle of a sentence and you realize at the end you're going to need to call up a certain word and you're worried you won't be able to, but you're already committed so you hurtle along and then pause because *you've* arrived at the end but the word hasn't? And it's not even a ten-dollar word you're after, like *polemic* or *shibboleth,* but a two-dollar word, like *distinctive,* so you just end up saying *amazing?*

Which is how you join the gang of nitwits who describe everything as *amazing.*

Well, it rattled the hell out of me. I had a memoir to write. Yes, much of my memoir was going to be illustrations. No problem there. The words were the rub. With a book, I couldn't just blather on in my accustomed way. Economy was everything. And economy wasn't happening due to the abovementioned bad brain.

I got the big idea to sharpen my instrument by memorizing poems. My mother was an actress; she used to recite Shakespeare soliloquies before bed. It was amazing. (There! *Amazing!* If my brain weren't so bad I might have said, *It was proof she was disciplined and properly educated and may have had an inkling of her terrible fate.*) So I did what anyone would do: I picked up the phone, called the University of Washington, and asked for their finest poetry teacher.

For the past year I've been meeting Alonzo Wrenn every Thursday morning at Lola for private lessons. He assigns me a poem. I recite it from memory, and the conversation gallops where it may. I pay him fifty bucks plus breakfast. Alonzo would buy *me* breakfast, so great is his love of poetry, but my will is stronger, so he accepts it and the crisp bill with a poet's grace.

"What did you think?" Alonzo asked.

He was a big guy, younger than me, with a mop of mouse-colored hair atop his exceedingly kind face. He always wore a suit, linen in the summer, wool in the winter. Today's was chocolate with a sheen; it must have been vintage, and under it a shirt the color of parchment. His tie was moiré, his pocket square starched white. (Joe's mother made him wear a suit and tie to the dentist to show "respect for the profession." Little Joe wearing a tie in the dentist's chair = falling in love all over.)

"Can we start with what's concretely happening in the poem?" I asked Alonzo. "What's the term for that? The discrete incident?"

"The discriminated occasion."

"The Discriminated Occasion!" I said. "You'd better make that the title of your autobiography."

"I might prefer *Discrete Incident.*"

I unfolded my marked-up poem and launched in. "It starts with the hermit heiress who lives year-round on the summer island. I'm picturing Maine."

Alonzo nodded, ceding it as a possibility.

" 'Her farmer,' " I said. "Is that her husband?"

"More like someone in her employ who farms her land."

"Like you're my poet," I said.

"Like I'm your poet."

"There's lots of oranges," I said. "But red too. Blue Hill is turning fox red. The red comes back later with the blood cells and the skunks' eyes. God, doesn't your heart break for the fairy decorator? Don't you just want to go buy something in his shop? Don't you want to just fix him up with the hermit heiress?"

"Now that you mention it," Alonzo said with a laugh.

"Then the poet steps out of the shadows. He's been saying 'our' up until now, but then it turns to 'I.' Is he called the poet or the narrator?"

"The narrator," Alonzo said.

"The narrator appears. It's a real shock when the poem alligator-tails around and says, 'My mind's not right.' "

"What do you know about Robert Lowell?" Alonzo asked.

"Only what you're about to tell me."

Our food arrived. Alonzo always ordered Tom's Big Breakfast. It comes with octopus *and* bacon. I always ordered the daily egg-white scramble with fruit. God, I depressed myself.

"Can I have your bacon?" I said.

"Robert Lowell was born to Boston Brahmins," Alonzo said, placing the thick strips on a saucer. "He battled mental illness his whole life and was in and out of institutions."

"Oh!" I suddenly had an idea. I waved over the waitress. "You know how you sell cookies and mints and that garlic spread? Can you make me a gift basket?"

For Sydney Madsen. Another bugbear was the way she always arrived with little presents for me. Today being different, I would bring her one too.

Alonzo continued. "The poet John Berryman suggests that 'Skunk Hour' depicts the moment when the 'I' of the poem —"

"The 'I' of the poem?" I had to laugh. "You're among friends. Just say it: Robert Lowell."

"When Robert Lowell recognizes a depression is coming on that will leave him hospitalized. 'A catatonic vision of frozen terror,' Berryman called this poem."

" 'I myself am hell; nobody's here. Only skunks,' " I said. Something occurred to me. "*Only.* Another one of our poems hinged on the word *only.*"

Alonzo frowned.

" 'Dover Beach'!" I practically shouted because how on earth did I remember that when I can't remember what year it is? " 'Come to the window, sweet is the night-air! *Only,* from the long line of spray'... That's when that poem turns on its axis too."

Alonzo pointed to my printout. "May I?"

"Go ahead."

He tore off a corner and wrote *only*.

"Look at me, making the page!" I said. "Will you use that in one of your poems?"

Alonzo cocked an eyebrow mysteriously and pulled out his wallet, bursting with similar scraps. Among the stacked credit cards, a blue stripe with white block letters—

"Hey," I said before I could think it through. "Why do you have a Louisiana driver's license?"

"It's where I grew up." Alonzo handed over a long-haired version of himself. "New Orleans."

With those two words: the sucker punch.

"Are you okay?" Alonzo asked.

"I've never been to Louisiana" were the words that came out, a bizarre nonanswer *and* a lie. Now I needed to say something true. "I have no connection to New Orleans."

Just hearing myself speak the name made me drop my fork into my breakfast.

The waitress bounced up with a gift basket the size of a car seat. "Someone's gonna be happy today!" Seeing my face, she quickly added, "Or not. We good here?"

"*I'm* good," Alonzo said.

"I'm good." To prove my point, I lifted my fork out of my eggs and gave the handle a defiant lick.

The waitress pivoted on her heel and scrammed.

"A question," I said, fumbling for the poem. I needed to get this morning back on track. "'Spar spire.' Would that be the steeple?"

"A spar is a ship's mast," Alonzo said. "So probably—"

My phone jumped to life. GALER STREET SCHOOL.

27

"There is no way," I said.

"Is this Eleanor? It's Lila from Galer Street. Everything's fine. It's just Timby seems to have a tummy ache."

Three times in the past two weeks I've had to pick him up early! Three times there was nothing wrong.

"Does he have a fever?" I asked.

"No, but he's looking awfully miserable lying here in the office."

"Please tell him to cut it out and go back to class."

"Ooh," Lila said. "But if he *is* sick..."

"That's what I'm telling you—" There was no arguing. "Okay, I'll be right there." I slid out of the booth. "That kid. I'll show him fear in a handful of dust."

I bade adieu to Alonzo, grabbed the gift basket, and split. As I opened the door, I glanced back. Alonzo, bless him, seemed more disconsolate than I that our poetry lesson had come to such an abrupt end.

I walked up the steps, between the thickset columns, and into the impressive foyer of the Galer Street School. It was underlit and cathedral cool. Framed photos told the story of the building's transformation from a home for wayward girls to a single-family residence (!) to today's ruinously expensive private school.

A little about the building's restoration. On the floor, in wood inlay, BECAUSE STRAIT IS THE GATE AND NARROW IS THE PATH WHICH LEADETH UNTO LIFE AND FEW THERE BE THAT FIND IT, dated to 1906. One hundred and fifty rubber molds were created for the intricate plaster work. Colorado alabaster was cut paper-thin for the clerestory. The mosaic of Christ teaching children to pray required flying in a seventy-year-old craftsman from Ravenna, Italy. When the restoration began in 2012, the big mystery was what had happened to the brass Art Deco chandelier from the early photos. It was found by the guys blowtorching blackberry vines out of the basement. Large blindfolded pigs were lowered in on ropes to chew the chandelier free.

How could I possibly know this? As I entered, the chic architect in charge of the restoration happened to be leading a tour.

On my way to the administration offices: "Eleanor!"

I turned. For the past month, the conference room had become auction central, abuzz with parent volunteers.

"You're just the person we need!" said the woman, a young mom.

Me? I mouthed, pointing, confused.

"Yes, you!" said another young mom as if I were a silly goose. "We have a question."

When I graduated from college it never would have occurred to me *not* to work. That's why women went to college, to get jobs. Get jobs we did and kicked some serious ass while we were at it, thank you very much, until we realized we'd lost track of time and madly scrambled to get pregnant. I pushed it dangerously close to the wire (no doubt because Catholic Joe, the oldest of seven, was in no hurry himself, having changed enough diapers for a lifetime). I gave birth to little Timby, thus joining the epidemic of haggard women in their forties trapped in playgrounds, slumped on boingy ladybugs, unconsciously pouring Tupperware containers of Cheerios down their own throats, donning maternity jeans two years after giving birth, and sporting skunk stripes down the center of their hair as they pushed swings. (Who needed to look good anymore? We got the kid!)

Was the sight of us so terrifying that the entire next generation of college-educated woman declared "Anything but that!" and forsook careers altogether to pop out children in their twenties? Looking at the Galer Street moms, the answer would be: Apparently.

I hope it works out for them.

I entered the conference room with its giant beveled windows overlooking the play yard and Elliott Bay. A massive table (cut from the center of a maple tree salvaged from the property or some such trendy nonsense, according to the architect) was piled with file boxes and cascading manila folders. I weaved my way through hip-height cardboard cartons with Galer Street T-shirts hanging out, red like tongues. The air crackled with efficiency and purpose.

"Where are you? Where are you? Where are you?" the young mom muttered.

"Here?" I said.

"You need to find the item number and cross-reference it with her name," said another young mom.

I went to Japan once and our guide claimed that to them, all Americans looked alike. At the time, I thought, Oh, you're just saying that about us because that's what we say about you. But beholding this array of young, glowing, physically fit moms, it occurred to me that Fumiko might not have been messing with me after all.

"Got ridiculous?" said the first young mom.

A young dad (because there's always one dad) held up a folder. "Victory is mine!"

"You won a latte, you won a latte," singsonged the first or the second or the third or the fourth mom.

Put these parents in a room with clerical work and zero supervision, and they start acting like the deranged winners in an Indian casino ad.

"You donated a hand-drawn portrait of the winning bidder in the style of *Looper Wash*," said one, finally acknowledging my existence.

"That's you?" asked another.

Like ostriches, they all stopped and cocked their heads at me.

"I heard you went here," said one, taking me in.

"Timby's mom," said another, the expert.

Seattle is short on star power. A past-her-prime animator and a Seahawks doctor make me and Joe the Galer Street equivalent of Posh and Becks.

"I'm a Vivian," said one.

"You're totally a Fern," corrected another.

"What are you doing *now?*" one flat-out asked me.

"I'm writing a memoir," I said, heat weirdly building in my cheeks. "A graphic memoir." It was none of their business, but I kept going. "I have an advance from a publisher and everything."

The ostriches smiled inscrutably.

On the table, a ring of keys. Each key had one of those color-coded rubber jobs around the top. In my life I'd bought a hundred of the damned things but had always given up because who can put them on without bending a nail? Also on the ring, a neat fan of bar-code tags from Breathe Hot Yoga, Core de Ballet, Spin Cycle…And in a personal touch, this young, fit mom had attached a lanyard with her child's name in baby blocks.

I turned my head sideways. What was the name?

D-E-L-P-H-I-N-E.

I froze.

"Yoo-hoo!" called a young mom.

"You forgot to put a dollar value as to what it's worth," said another.

"What what's worth?" I said, snapping to.

"Your auction item," put in another. "For tax purposes."

"Oh. I don't know."

"We need to put down something," said the first young mom.

"It's just a few hours of my time." My breath had become stuck. Why did I have to see those goddamned keys?

"What's your time worth?" This was the young dad, wresting control.

"Literally?" I said. "Per hour?"

Did he mean the hours I spent lying in bed vowing to change?

The hours shopping for organizers that forever remained in the bags? The hours researching mindfulness classes, signing up for them, going so far as parking outside art-gallery-yoga-studios and watching the well-intentioned students file in, only to lose my nerve and peel out? The hours planning to eat dinner as a family, just to end up hunched in front of our screens, every man for himself? The hours steeped in shame that I had no excuse for any of it?

And then, squeals.

The first-graders had burst onto the lawn wearing butterfly wings shellacked with colorful bits of tissue paper. The young moms (and the one dad) turned their backs to me and basked in the slipstream of their children's spontaneity and delight. The energy in the room shifted from bubbly conviviality to hushed reverence. All the choices these young moms (and the one dad) had agonized over — to work or not work, to marry young or keep looking, to have a kid now or see the world first — had led to hard decisions. And with decisions come regrets. And sleepless nights, and recriminations, and fights with their husbands (and the one wife), and whacked-out calls to the doctor for pills. The "catatonic vision of frozen terror" the poet had called these moments of existential doubt, or certainty, it was hard to know which. But seeing their children now, in this instant, these parents knew in their teeth that their decisions had been the right ones.

So, with a perfectly timed cough, I grabbed that young mom's ring of keys, dropped them in my purse, and slipped out.

That's right, I stole them.

Timby was lying on a cot in a corner of the office looking, to my trained eye, pretty darned pleased with himself.

"Get up," I said. "I'm officially sick of this BS."

On the downside, I'd said that. On the upside, it was so unnecessarily nasty that Lila and the other administrators pretended not to hear. Timby darkened and followed me out.

I waited until we were standing at the car. "We're going straight to the doctor's. And you'd better pray there's really something wrong with you."

"Can't we just go home?"

"So you can drink ginger ale and watch *Doctor Who*? No. I refuse to reward you any more for faking stomachaches. We're going to the doctor and straight back to school." I leaned in close. "And for all I know, it's time for you to get a shot."

"You're mean."

We got in the car.

"What's this?" Timby asked with big eyes upon seeing the gift basket.

"Not for you. Don't get your paws near that thing."

Timby was crying now. "You're getting mad at me for being sick."

We drove to the pediatrician's in silence, me angry at Timby, me angry with myself for being angry at Timby, me angry at Timby, me angry with myself for being angry at Timby.

His little voice: "I love you, Mom."

"I love you too."

"Timby?" said the nurse. "That's an unusual name."

"I was named by an iPhone," Timby said around the thermometer in his mouth.

"*I* named you," I said.

"No." Timby glared.

"Yes." I glared back.

When I was pregnant, we learned it was going to be a boy. Joe and I ecstatically volleyed names back and forth. One day I texted *Timothy*, which autocorrected to *Timby*. How could we not?

The nurse pulled out the thermometer. "Normal. The doctor will be right in."

"Nice work," I said after she left, "making me look bad."

"It's true," Timby said. "And why would an iPhone autocorrect a normal name to a name nobody's ever heard of?"

"It was a bug," I said. "It was the first iPhone—oh God!" I'd just realized. "I think I insulted Alonzo."

"How?" Timby looked all sweet but I knew he just wanted to lure me in for ammo to use against me.

"Nothing," I said.

It was the look on Alonzo's face as I left the restaurant. Maybe he *wasn't* sad to see me go. Maybe he was insulted that I'd called him "my poet."

Timby hopped off the table and opened the door.

"Where are you going?" I asked.

"To get a magazine." The door slammed.

My phone rang: *Joyce Primm*. As usual, 10:15 on the dot. I turned off the ringer and stared at the name.

You know me from *Looper Wash*. And yes, I'm responsible for giving the show its retro-violent and sherbet-colored aesthetic. (I'd long been obsessed with the outsider artist Henry Darger. Lucky me, I bought one of his paintings while they were still affordable.) I'll even concede that in the pilot script, the four lead girls were flat on the page. It was only when I dressed them in '60s-style pinafores, gave them tangled hair, and, just for fun, put them on bored ponies that the writer, Violet Parry, understood what the show could be. She did a feverish rewrite and gave the girls nasty right-wing personalities, thus transforming them into the fabled Looper Four, who misdirected their unconscious fear of puberty into a random hatred of hippies, owners of purebred dogs, and babies named Steve. That said, *Looper Wash* wasn't *mine*. Nobody's ever heard of Eleanor Flood.

I'd been semi-working, semi-broke, and living in New York. A children's catalog I'd illustrated caught the eye of Violet, who took a gutsy gamble and made me her animation director.

The first thing I learned about TV: It's all about the deadlines. An episode not being ready for air? It could not happen, not even once. Settling for uninspired angles, hacky hand gestures, mismatched lip flap, wonky eyes, excessive cycling of backgrounds, signs misspelled by foreign animators, color errors? Oh, that happened plenty. But it would never occur to even the laziest, craziest animation director not to turn in the show on time.

Publishing, on the other hand...

While my name meant nothing, my style was instantly recognizable. And for a while, *Looper Wash* was everywhere. A rising-star book editor named Joyce Primm (that's right, Joyce Primm, circling around, a method to the madness) had seen some drawings I'd done of my childhood and gave me an advance to expand them into a memoir.

I'm a little past my deadline.

For the longest time I didn't hear a peep from Joyce. But here she was, calling every day for the past week.

My phone stopped ringing. Her voice mail joined the boneyard of other voice mails.

JOYCE PRIMM
JOYCE PRIMM
JOYCE PRIMM
JOYCE PRIMM
JOYCE PRIMM

All with little blue dots, none I dared listen to.

Timby returned with a *People* magazine. On the cover, someone I didn't recognize, no doubt a reality-TV star.

"They should rename it *Who Are These People?*" I said.

"I've heard of him," Timby said, hurt on behalf of the famous person.

"That's even more depressing," I said.

"Knock, knock!" It was the pediatrician, Dr. Saba, her disposition even gentler than the nurse's.

"So, Timby," she said, disinfecting her hands. "I hear you have a tummy ache."

"This is the third time in two weeks I've had to pick him—"

"Let's hear it from Timby," the doctor said with a forgiving smile.

Timby addressed the floor. "My stomach aches."

"Is it all the time?" Dr. Saba asked. "Or just sometimes?"

"Sometimes."

"And you're in third grade?"

"Yes."

"What school do you go to?"

"Galer Street."

"Do you like it?"

"I guess."

"Do you have friends?"

"I guess."

"Do you like your teachers?"

"I guess."

"Timby." Dr. Saba wheeled up on a stool. "A lot of times when people get tummy aches, it's not because they have a bug, but because they have emotions that make them feel yucky."

Timby's eyes remained down.

"I'm wondering if there's anything going on at school or at home that's making you feel yucky."

Good luck with that, I thought. Timby, the king of the nonanswer.

"It's Piper Veal."

(!!!)

"Who's Piper Veal?" the doctor said.

"A new girl in my class."

Piper's family was fresh from a yearlong trip around the world. Is this not a rarefied but most annoying trend? Families traveling around the world to unplug and immerse themselves in foreign cultures, then parents frantically e-mailing you to please post comments on their kids' blogs so they won't think nobody gives a hoot? (Come on, *New York Times*, do I have to come up with all your most-e-mailed articles?)

"What's Piper doing?" asked Dr. Saba.

"She's bullying me," Timby said, his voice cracking.

My life zoomed into awful focus.

Here, now, Timby.

The gentleness, the celebrity gossip, the overidentification with Gaston from *Beauty and the Beast*. Was Timby gay? It had certainly occurred to me. But there were also the Snap Circuits, *MythBusters*, the obsession with escalators. Of course, the smoking gun would be the flirtation with makeup, but that was his Pavlovian response to being loved up by a harem of Nordstrom hotties. If anything, it proved Timby was all man. A mother knows. Or, in my case, a mother will love him regardless and let it play out the way it's going to play out.

Which is more than I can say for Galer Street.

Our first interview, we'd come straight from Nordstrom, where the girls had adorned Timby with a beauty mark and very subtle mascara...darling! As soon as we walked in the conference room, I could practically hear the admissions director shouting, "Eureka! We've got a transgender!" Joe and I joked about it later that night. After we'd been accepted, and without telling us, the school had taken it upon themselves to switch all the boys' and girls' bathrooms to gender-neutral. "I hope you didn't do this for Timby," I said to the head of school, Gwen. "Oh no," she said. "We did it for all our little genderqueers."

To that, there could be only one response: to laugh my ass off. But I had the good sense to wait until I got outside.

Was I in denial? Had I become lulled into complacency as a reaction against Galer Street's fervent embrace of everything? And just because the administrators were so tolerant of the occasional pink thumbnail, the same might not be said for the kids on the playground...

"Have you told your mom about Piper?" asked Dr. Saba.

"No," Timby said.

Dr. Saba didn't have to shoot me a disappointed look. I could feel it beaming through the back of her skull.

"Have you told your teachers?"

"No."

"What kind of things is Piper doing to you?"

"I don't know," Timby said.

"Is she hurting your body?" Dr. Saba asked.

"No," Timby said, his mouth full of saliva.

"What did Piper do?"

I twisted in my chair and held my breath.

"She told me I bought my shirt at H&M."

Oh.

"You bought your shirt at H&M?" repeated the doctor.

"When Piper was in Bangladesh she went on a tour of a factory with child slaves and they were making clothes for H&M."

"I see," said Dr. Saba. "Timby, third grade is when things start to get complicated with your friends. Sometimes your feelings can get so big they cause a tummy ache."

Timby finally looked up and into Dr. Saba's eyes.

"Do you know the best medicine for that?" she asked.

"What?"

"Talk to your grown-up," Dr. Saba said. "Your mom. But if it's not your mom—"

"It is his mom," I said.

"—talk to your dad, your grandma, your favorite teacher. Tell them how you're feeling. They might not be able to fix it, but sometimes just talking is enough."

Timby smiled.

"You look like you're feeling better already."

"I am."

"That's what I like to hear," she said, standing.

"Good," I said. "We can go back to school."

Timby hopped off the table and pulled open the door.

"Hey, where's he going?" I asked.

The door shut. It was just me, Dr. Saba, and the mural of zombie-eyed lemurs.

"Do you have to go right back to work?" Dr. Saba asked. "Because what Timby really needs is mommy time."

"I'll move some stuff around."

Dr. Saba stood there, calling my bluff. I dialed Sydney Madsen and got voice mail. "Sydney. I have to reschedule. Something came up with Timby."

Dr. Saba gave me a nod and headed out.

Timby was at the nurses' station, whistling as he ferreted through a cardboard box covered with wrapping paper.

A nurse asked, "Do you want a *Wash Your Hands* pencil or a *Good Job* tattoo?"

"Can I have both?" Timby said, still scrounging. "Ooh, is this gum?" He picked up a box but dropped it instantly when it turned out to be chalk.

That was it. Timby was going back to school. And I was going to get this Sydney Madsen lunch behind me. The last thing I needed was a fresh round of passive-aggressive subject lines: "Remember Me?" "Hello, Stranger!" "Lunch with a Friend?"

(So needy! As far as I'm concerned, the only thing sweeter than seeing a friend is that friend canceling on me.)

I dialed Sydney's number. "Hi! Forget my last message. I'll see you at noon—"

Somehow Dr. Saba was standing there.

"—some other day. Just making sure you got the message."

"Am I going back to school or not?" Timby asked.

The spotlight was on me.

"We're going to have some mommy time!" I said.

"Mommy time?" he said, not unafraid.

We left Dr. Saba's office and stepped onto the streets of downtown, my mind a muddle. What I needed now was Joe. Joe could cut through my confusion. Joe the sword.

There's a phenomenon I call the Helpless Traveler. If you're traveling with someone who's confident, organized, and decisive you become the Helpless Traveler: "Are we there yet?" "My bags are too heavy." "My feet are getting blisters." "This isn't what I ordered." We've all been that person. But if the person you're traveling with is helpless, then *you* become the one able to decipher train schedules, spend five hours walking on marble museum floors without complaint, order fearlessly from foreign menus, and haggle with crooked cabdrivers. Every person has it in him to be either the Competent Traveler or the Helpless Traveler. Because Joe is so clearheaded and sharp, I've been able to go through life as the Helpless Traveler. Which, now that I think about it, might not be such a good thing. It's a question for Joe.

His office was a few blocks away. Even just seeing him through the glass would be enough to center me.

"Wait," Timby said. "We're going to Dad's? Can I play with the iPad?"

Joe and I were waging the altogether futile war against electronics by not letting Timby play video games. The one loophole was the iPads in Joe's office.

"Is that something you'd like to do?" I asked Timby in an unexpected singsong, like a stranger offering candy. "I could drop you off while I popped over to lunch."

"Whoa," he said, processing his unbelievably good fortune. "Yeah!"

I called Sydney yet again.

"Guess who? Disregard my messages. I'll see you at noon!"

"Hey, look!" Timby had spotted the sign for Jazz Alley. "It's that place with the oily hummus and they make ginger ale by combining Coke and Sprite, and you have to sit at tiny tables smooshed together with people you don't know."

Perhaps I'd complained more than once about being dragged there by jazz-loving Joe. If you were ever driven to the brink of madness listening to Rush's "Tom Sawyer," try sitting through an aggro jazz trio doing a baffling forty-five-minute version.

"I'm not a fan of jazz," I said to Timby. "No woman is."

"You should tell Dad to go by himself," he said.

"Don't think I haven't tried," I said. "But there's something about me the guy can't quit."

We shared a shrug and headed to Joe's office.

＊

The first thing that should have tripped my alarm was the empty waiting room. But this wasn't completely unprecedented. Joe had celebrity clients (athletes and musicians) who, for a variety of reasons (ego and ego), couldn't be in the same waiting room as civilians. Therefore, down the hall from the double-doored entrance to the Wallace Surgery Center was a row of single, unmarked private waiting rooms. Conceivably, Joe's patients could have been in there.

The second thing I noticed, which did trip my alarm, was the top of the aquarium lying across the couch.

In defense of celebrities (!), they all love Joe. No matter how coddled the quarterback or preening the guitarist, as soon as something goes wrong with their hand, they fly to Seattle because they've heard about The Guy. When The Guy turns out to be unpretentious Joe, they become smitten. Joe waters the plants himself. His desk is a mess. The office is in constant chaos because he spends too long with each patient. He treats everyone the same, his curiosity a gentle rain. You'd have to draw him a picture to explain why it's cooler to save the pinkie of a Cy Young Award–winning pitcher than the wrist of a checkout lady with carpal tunnel. Stars *like* the people who fawn over them; they *trust* the few who don't.

Nobody was behind the reception window. I moved closer. On the desk was an open container of tortellini salad, its bottled Italian dressing a Proustian blast back to a past I wanted no part of: broke, in New York, eating Korean-deli salad bar.

Deep in the office, Luz the receptionist caught sight of me. I waved. Luz walked over, wiping her hands on her jeans. Jeans + stinky desk food = three-alarm situation.

Luz slid the glass over. "You're back!"

One thing that happens when you have an alcoholic for a parent is you grow up the child of an alcoholic. For those of you who aren't children of alcoholics, hear me now and believe me later: It's the single determining factor in your personality. I don't care if you get straight As, marry a saint, and break the glass ceiling in a male-dominated profession, or if you bounce around from failure to failure with pit stops in cults and nuthouses: if you were raised by a drunk, you're above all the adult child of an alcoholic. For a quick trip around the bases, it means you blame yourself for everything, you avoid reality, you can't trust people, you're hungry to please. Which isn't all bad: perfectionism makes the straight-A student; lack of trust begets self-sufficiency; low self-esteem can be a terrific motivator; if everyone were so gung-ho on reality, there'd be no art.

An added bonus of having a drunk for a father is that in order to survive, I became freakishly attuned to subtle body language and inflections. Joe calls this heightened perception my "witchly powers."

And right then, to anybody else, "You're back!" would have meant *Nice to see you! It's been a while.* But to the child of an alcoholic with witchly powers, it meant *Joe told us the three of you were out of town.*

And that's when my day really began.

Ruthie, in the way back, spotted us. Ruthie the office manager and Luz the scheduler were a pair of evil cats. Placid eyes, grins seething with calculation, they worked in tandem with a single purpose: to protect Joe.

Ruthie, the mastermind, was sixty, blond, with a dancer's body. She always wore beige. Today's ensemble was a silk top, pointy four-inch heels, and slacks with a crease down the front that could slice you in half.

I wanted information. If I tipped Ruthie off, she'd run straight to Joe. My witchly instincts told me that whatever this was—Joe telling me he was at work but the office he was out of town—I needed to low-key it.

Evil cats versus the adult child of an alcoholic. May the better animal win.

"This is a surprise," Ruthie said, revealing nothing.

"We're back," I said, safe ground, as I was merely repeating what Luz had just said.

Two workmen walked through the back hallway. Propped against the wall, a roll of carpet.

"New carpet?" I said.

"We never have a whole week!" erupted Luz.

A whole week? Hmm.

Ruthie put her hand on Luz's shoulder. A signal to say no more?

What was that I sensed from four feet away? Could it be Ruthie's heart rate dropping? Had the kitty cat checkmated me?

"I parked in the garage," I said.

Then, in a prison move if there ever was one, I reached across and rifled around Luz's desk, touching as much of her personal shit as I could.

An appalled Luz turned to Ruthie, who coolly opened a drawer and handed me validation stickers.

"Take the whole book," she said.

Timby was up on a chair with both hands in the aquarium, swishing his fingers through the fetid water. "Whee!"

"Let's go," I said.

Out in the hallway, I found a wall-mounted hand-sanitizer dispenser. Trembling, I pushed the button. It squirted on the floor. I scooped up the puff of foam and knelt down to scrub it into Timby's arms.

"Oh no," he cried. "Was that water dirty?"

"Not necessarily."

"Smell the soup, cool the soup," Timby said.

"Huh?"

"It's what they teach us in school when we're upset. Smell the soup." He took a deep breath in. "Cool the soup." He blew out. "Come on, Mama, close your eyes."

I stood up. Eyes closed, I smelled the soup. I cooled the soup. My arms rose slightly at my sides; my palms turned inward on their own; my fingers curled like fortune-telling fish.

"I think I need moisturizer," Timby said, his arms pink from the alcohol.

"We'll get you some, baby."

I dialed Sydney. "Eleanor again. This really is the last time. But I do have to cancel. Call me so I know you got this message."

I turned to Timby. "Me and you."

"Really?" His fragile hope just about put me away.

"What do you want to do?" I said. "Anything. We can go paddleboarding on Lake Union. Get a sandwich to eat at the top of Smith Tower. Fly kites on Kite Hill. Watch the salmon swim upstream at the Ballard Locks."

"Can we go to the Gap?"

To the Gap we walked.

"This is all about you, baby," I said.

Timby tore up the Lucite stairs to the kids' section. I followed him, my mind barely there.

Husband caught lying = husband having an affair. It felt like a first idea; it felt pat.

My friend Merrill told me that on the first date, a guy without realizing it will tell you why the relationship will ultimately fail. He'll say he doesn't want kids, or he's not the type to settle down, or he's in a fight with his mother. On our first date, Joe presented himself as the kind, curious, principled man he turned out to be.

Only one thing struck me as odd.

I don't know how it came up. But he said his coping style was that he takes it, he takes it, he takes it, until he can't take it anymore. "What does it look like, when you can't take it anymore?" I'd asked. "I don't know," he'd answered. "It hasn't happened yet."

The previous guy I'd dated was still hung up on his ex. The one before him was fifteen days sober. If the worst Joe could say about himself was there'd be unspecified wall-punching in the future, sign me up! (And even that didn't materialize! Twenty years and nary a call to the drywall guy.)

More than anything, Joe is ethical. I once pointed out the irony of him constantly railing against the Catholic Church when he is in fact a walking advertisement for the decency and honesty they preach. ("When they're not pumping you with lies and self-hatred," he'd retorted.)

No way could he be cheating on me.

On the other hand, I wasn't giving him enough sex. I had to get on that.

I poked my head into the dressing room. Timby was trying on corduroy shorts and a T-shirt of a corgi playing drums. Timby's roll of dimpled, paper-white belly fat popped out over the waistband.

"Do you think they have kneesocks?" he asked.

Not in the boys' section! I knew not to say.

And then I remembered. This morning. Joe facedown at the table, forehead on the *newspaper*. Perhaps he'd seen something in it...

"I'm running across the street to Barnes and Noble just for a sec."

"Wait," Timby said. "You're leaving me here alone?"

Before I could fumble for an answer, he said, "Can I pick out something else?" The kid had a gambler's instinct for knowing when to press.

"One thing."

I shot to the bookstore, bought a *Seattle Times,* and hustled outside. In the few minutes that took, a stack of wooden barricades had appeared on the sidewalk. Seattle was breaking out in a rash of police blue.

Did I fail to mention that the Pope was coming to town? Oh yeah. For something called World Youth Day. (Does that not sound like a bogus event the Joker would dream up to ensnare Robin?) His Holiness was scheduled to perform Mass at the Mariners stadium on Saturday.

I thumbed through the newspaper. Seahawks, Seahawks, Seahawks. Pope, Pope, Pope. A lady was setting out food for crows, and her neighbors were pissed. Any of these could have driven Joe to despair. Or none.

What a royal frustration! Of course I hadn't pushed it this morning with Joe. Isn't that one of the benefits of plodding through so many years of marriage? You get to take things at face value? None of that "You look upset," "I'm not upset," "Please talk to me," "I am talking to you," "Is it me?," "I told you I'm fine," "It *is* me." Oy, just thinking about it takes me back to Friday nights spent weeping through step class.

By the time I got back to the Gap, Timby had pulled a *Supermarket Sweep.* A girl with a headset was ringing up a haystack of clothes.

Between scanner beeps, Timby whispered, "Hurry, hurry."

"Don't think you got away with this," I said, coming up behind him. "I know you tricked me."

"Will you be using your Gap card today?" the girl asked.

"No, and I don't want one," I said. "We're never coming back."

"You ruin everything," Timby said.

"No, *you* ruin everything."

The salesgirl's smile didn't falter, but that didn't mean she couldn't wait to get home and tell her roommate.

It was 11:45 and still no word from Sydney. Out on the street, a white police bus had parked across Sixth Avenue, blocking traffic. I dialed Sydney's number. As it rang, I pointed to the bus.

"Look," I said to Timby. "The Pope must be staying at the Sheraton. That's what you get when you call yourself the People's Pope. You have to stay at a dump."

"I wish *I* could stay at the Sheraton."

Voice mail again. "Sydney? It's Eleanor. Please call me. I don't want you showing up at lunch and I'm not there. Or maybe I should go. I don't know." I hung up. "See, this is why I can't stand Sydney Madsen."

"I thought she was your friend."

"It's a grown-up thing." I pulled the newspaper from under my arm and pointed to the date. "Read that to me."

Timby did.

I handed him my date book. "Look up today. Thursday, October eighth. Tell me what it says."

"Spencer Martell."

"Give me that." I yanked away the book. In my own hand: SPENCER MARTELL.

"Who's Spencer Martell?" Timby asked.

"I can't imagine."

Spencer Martell. Whoever it was, I had made a lunch date with...him? Her?

"Who's Spencer Martell?" Timby asked again.

"Do I look like I know?"

"It's okay, Mom," he said. "You did it on accident."

"It's 'by accident.' Who's teaching you to speak?"

I took out my phone and searched *Spencer Martell*. One e-mail came up from a month ago.

From: Spencer Martell
To: Eleanor Flood
Re: Long time no see!
By any chance are you free for lunch on October 8? I'd love to catch up.
xS

I scrolled down and found my response. A twelve o'clock reservation at Mamnoon.

It was now ten of.

"Maybe he's related to Sydney Madsen," Timby offered. "He could be her brother."

"We're about to find out, aren't we?"

"I'm coming too?" Timby said with big eyes.

"Me and you."

As for my constant low-grade state of confusion—the Blur is a term that seems to be sticking—let me break it into three categories: (1) things I should know but never learned, (2) things I choose not to know, and (3) things I know but totally screw up.

Things I should know but never learned? My left from my right. Sorry, but you better ask someone else for directions.

Things I choose not to know? Plenty. There's only so much a good brain has room for, let alone a bad brain like mine. So I made an executive decision: There would be subjects I'd aggressively take no interest in, such as the Israeli-Palestinian conflict, Lena Dunham, the whereabouts of the stolen paintings from the Isabella Stewart Gardner heist, what GMO even stands for, and, until Timby's flirtation with kneesocks in the Gap five minutes ago, gender identity. If that makes my human existence a limited one, I stoically accept my fate. Today's prevailing stance seems to be *I have an opinion, therefore I am.* My stance? *I have no opinion, therefore I am superior to you.*

Things I know but always screw up? Times. If I have a lunch at 12:30, I'll write *12:30* in my book. But along the way, some alchemy happens in my brain and 12:30 becomes 1:00. You'd think that after arriving for the theater half an hour after curtain (a dozen times!), I'd have learned to triple-check the ticket. But no. I wish I could explain it. One of life's enigmas.

My point is, switching Spencer Martell to Sydney Madsen might send *you* running to the neurologist, but to me it's a shrug-fest.

✳

A parking space gaped across the street from the restaurant. What if this was my only karmic blessing of the day? I almost hated to waste it.

"This is going to be a grown-up lunch, you understand that," I said, sticking the parking receipt on the inside of the window.

"Will it be inappropriate?" Timby asked, climbing out of the car hugging the gift basket.

"We're going to talk about what we're going to talk about, and you'll have to sit there. To nip it in the bud, in terms of can-we-go-nows, the answer is no."

"What if there's an earthquake?"

"What did I say?"

"Can I listen to the radio on your phone?"

"No. But I do have those books on tape."

"It's all Laura Ingalls Wilder."

"You've been ruined by *Literally Not Even*," I said.

"What's *Literally Not Even*?"

"That horrible show you're always watching."

"It's called *I Know, Right?*"

"Then *I Know, Right?* has totally ruined you," I said.

"God, Mom," Timby said. "You've never even seen it."

"Don't listen to anything," I said. "Just sit there."

"Fine," Timby said bitterly. "Laura Ingalls Wilder."

While we waited to cross the street, a homeless guy passed by. White with dreads, a beard, and red everything: skin, eyes, peeling hands, tops of his bare feet. His face, his whole body, searched for something, anything.

"Come here." I pulled Timby in.

"Is he mentally ill?"

"I just want to hold you close." I gave Timby a squeeze. He relaxed in my embrace. "I'm wild about you, you know that, right?"

"I know." He smiled up at me.

"You don't have to be wild about me too. Just try to like me a little more than you do now."

We entered Mamnoon with its ebony walls, industrial ceiling, fabulous bursts of geometric mosaic, and whimsical, but not too whimsical, chandeliers. I don't care where you live, but here in Seattle, our restaurants are better than your restaurants.

"Hmmm," I said. "Who are we looking for?"

"Spencer Martell," Timby said.

"I know that," I snapped.

Deep in the restaurant, a man stood and waved. Thirties, skinny, he wore a yellow gingham shirt, a brown belt, and black jeans.

"There he is," I said, waving back. "I know him…"

"From where?" Timby asked.

Fifteen steps away, he looked familiar. Eight steps away, and I almost remembered… And there we were.

"Spencer!"

"Eleanor," he said, with deep affection.

"You!"

Timby shot me a look: *Who is it?* I shot him one back: *Don't ask me.*

"Is this your son?" Spencer asked.

"You've met?" I said, not sure.

"We brought you a basket," Timby said.

"If I'd known you were coming," Spencer said to Timby, hands on bent knees, "I'd have brought you something too."

Timby did the math quicker than Bobby Fischer and spotted a leather case on the table. He grabbed it and snapped it open.

On a bed of satin rested an orange Montblanc pen, the kind I used to use, the kind they stopped making forever ago.

"The rollerball," Spencer said to me. "If I remember correctly."

"I can't believe you found one." The weight of it, the unlikeliness of its clownish color, the double-click of the top coming off and on in my hand. "On eBay I can only find midnight blue—"

"And teal," Spencer jumped in. "And forest green and yellow."

"But orange," I said. "This is precious cargo."

"I want to see!" Timby grabbed the pen.

"How wonderful and unexpected." I looked Spencer in the eye. "Thank you."

"How do you know my mom?" Timby, my wingman.

Before he could open his mouth, Gah!

Spencer Martell!

From *Looper Wash*!

It had been over ten years since he'd shambled out of the office.

"I worked with your mom a long time ago." The warmth in his voice belied the ugly memory that was reloading in my brain with alarming speed.

When Spencer walked into the bullpen that first day, he looked the part: Moleskine notebook, Blackwing pencils, vintage glasses. He dropped the names of the right artists: Robert Williams, Alex Grey, Tara McPherson, Adrian Tomine.

However...

He was so nervous and eager to ingratiate himself that his presence was excruciating. He'd arrive each Monday having scoured Brooklyn swap meets for items we animators might add to our various collections. I mentioned once that I liked caramel brownies and the next day he brought in a tray, homemade...

How could I have even hired him? Oh, that's right! I didn't hire him! We got him for free, through the network's minority hiring program. Then it turned out he was just a quarter Mexican and that he'd gamed the system to get the job! Oh, and he couldn't even draw! He kept badgering me with questions about every tiny gesture and expression. *I* wasn't there to help *him*. *He* was there to help *me*. I needed people to shut up, churn out drawings, and stick to the model sheet.

Spencer quickly realized he was in over his head; his flop sweat made him radioactive. When his eight-week option was up, his spirit was so broken that he'd already packed his boxes. He sat in his empty office waiting to get fired. I gutlessly made someone else do it. But Spencer didn't come out for an hour. The only sign he was alive was sobbing through the door. I went in. I gave him some career advice. It came out wrong.

I waved over the first person dressed in black. "We need to order."

"We do?" Timby said.

I turned to Spencer. "And just so you know—"

"You don't share," he said. "I remember."

"Can I get two things?" Timby asked.

"One."

We ordered. And there we were, me, Timby and my quarter-Mexican, nattily attired Ghost of Christmas Past mooning at me from across the table. Someone had to say something.

"Spencer Martell!"

"I can't believe you answered my e-mail," he said. "I'd always assumed you'd rather forget me."

"Of course not," I said with an insouciant wave that knocked my water into the dipping oil.

Timby was starting to look concerned.

Spencer mopped up the water with his napkin and moved his phone to the dry side.

It gave me an idea.

"Timby," I said. "Go wash your hands."

"But—"

"Fish poop," I said. "Or you're not eating French fries, and they have the best French fries."

Timby burned me with a stare and left.

"Spencer." I leaned across the table. "If I dial a number from your cell phone, will you try to make a doctor's appointment?"

"Uh—" The poor guy looked poleaxed.

I'd already grabbed his phone and dialed Joe's office. "I don't want them to know it's me. Just ask when the next available appointment is." I held Spencer's phone to his ear.

I could hear Luz answer. I motioned wildly for Spencer to start talking.

"Yes—hello—" he stammered. "I'd like to make an appointment."

Luz explained something on the other end.

"Ask when he's coming back," I whispered.

"When's he coming back?" Spencer said weakly.

"Monday," said Luz.

That's all I needed to know. I snatched the phone from Spencer, hung it up, and placed it on the table.

He looked down at it, then up at me, uncertain if the last minute had actually happened.

"Dr. Wallace..." Spencer said. "Isn't that your husband? Joe? Are you divorced?"

"Pshaw. We're happily married."

Timby slid back in beside a thoroughly charmed or slightly disgusted Spencer, it was hard to tell which.

I'm kidding! He was disgusted.

"Spencer," I said. "Tell us about you."

"Well, that's a three-hour tour!" he said, reassuming his happy-to-be-here persona.

"The abridged version will do," I said.

"When I left *Looper Wash*..."

I had to heave my breath up and out. "I was trying to be helpful."

"What did you do?" Timby asked.

"It's not important," I said.

"The difficult people are our most valuable teachers," Spencer said.

"What did she do to you?" Timby was dying.

"Don't you have music to listen to?" I said.

"I'm good."

Spencer pulled out a stylish messenger bag and opened it for Timby. "I have some picture books you can look at," he said, placing a few on the bench between them.

Timby ignored the offer and raised his eyebrows as if to say, *You may proceed.*

"When I got hired at *Looper Wash*," Spencer said, "it was the happiest day of my life. I thought I'd arrived. I moved out of my parents' apartment in Queens. I bought a Vespa. I spent all my money on gifts for the other animators."

"Which I, for one, really appreciated. That signed Stephen Sondheim *Playbill* is still one of my most treasured possessions." I held my hand to my face to block even a peripheral view of Timby.

"Then I got fired. The shame of it. There I was, living in the East Village in an apartment I couldn't afford. I couldn't face my parents. For the first time in my life I wasn't sharing a bedroom with five brothers and sisters, and I could finally act on the fact that...I..." He looked at Timby, unsure. "Didn't like girls."

"He knows all about it." I flipped my head toward Timby. "I let him watch the Tonys."

"Oh. Well, the first guy I fell in love with was a drug addict, the hard stuff. Quicker than you might imagine, I ended up broke and with nowhere to live. But no matter how low I sank, I knew I was an artist. Despite what you said, I knew I was more than a careerist."

I'd called him that. I was hoping he'd forgotten.

"What's a careerist?" asked Timby.

"I had to look it up too," Spencer said. "It's someone who only thinks about getting ahead in his or her career."

"That's not bad," Timby said, disappointed.

Spencer put his hand to his heart. "Even now, when I think back on *Looper Wash*, the pangs of humiliation can make me drop the glass in my hand. I was so naive, such an embarrassment to myself."

"Not at all," I said. "It just wasn't the right fit."

"You had nowhere to live," Timby prompted helpfully.

"I'd lost all belief in myself," Spencer said. "But something deep within kept me going. A feeling of hope. And that hope was a pulsing, radiant green."

"Green hope!" I cried.

"It was the tip of a crocus breaking through in the winter. It was the shag carpet in the basement of a ranch house. It was the lace on my sister's *quinceañera* dress. Stop me if you've already heard this."

"Me?" I coughed, completely baffled as to how I could have.

"If I captured those greens," Spencer said, "it would release the artist who'd been taken hostage by the careerist." He unbuttoned his shirt cuffs, held together by silk French knots. He rolled up his sleeves and brandished his inner arms. On each, a tattoo from wrist to elbow: green paint-sample strips.

"Whoa," said Timby.

"That's quite a commitment," I said, then noticed his watch: vintage Cartier.

"I refused to let my failure at *Looper Wash* define me," Spencer said. "I spent my last dollar on a painting at a thrift shop just for the canvas, painted it green, and while the paint was still wet, cried onto it."

"Oy," I said.

"Mom! You're mean."

Spencer removed the napkin from his lap, folded it, and placed it on the table. He stood up and walked over to me. Were my arms shielding my face? Maybe. But instead of striking me, Spencer hugged me. It took breathing exercises from childbirth class to survive his bewildering, tuberose-scented act of compassion.

Timby, traumatized, gave me a look: *What's he doing?*

I gave him one back: *No idea.*

Spencer returned to his seat. Timby handed him his napkin. There was no choice now but to respect the dude.

"You're right," Spencer said. "It was sentimental and muddled. But it was the first true thing I'd ever done. That painting is here in Seattle. I'd love to show it to you."

"I want to see it!" Timby said.

"Read a book."

"Listen to me!" Spencer smacked his forehead. "I promised I'd make it short. So I came out, became a junkie, got these tattoos, cleaned up, and, well, you know about the past twelve years."

"I do?"

"Yale School of Art, group show at White Columns, Jack Wolgin Prize, Venice Biennale, blah-blah-blah."

My eyes closed; my face scrunched; my head shook a thousand tiny times. "Huh?"

"I thought you knew about me," Spencer said. To Timby: "Your mom—"

But Timby had become absorbed in one of Spencer's books.

Spencer turned back to me. "That's why I crave you, Eleanor. You have a way of frying my motherboard when I need it the most."

"It's not intentional!" I said. "I promise."

"The contemporary art world is so insular. We think our sky-high prices make us the center of the universe when of course only about eight people are paying attention. And they're just gallery owners and art consultants." Spencer joined his hands and lowered his chest in a slight bow. "I honor you."

"That's you?" I said, still gaga. "Yale, Venice?"

"I'm having a solo show at the Seattle Art Museum," he said. "They asked me to do some stuff at the sculpture park too. There are banners all over town. Of course I just presumed you saw my name flapping in the breeze everywhere you went. But here you are again, holding up the mirror."

This toadying wannabe, this sweaty ass-kisser, this fraudulent quasi-minority, now he was *somebody*? Now he was the shit? He'd turned everything topsy-turvy and instead of rubbing my face in it, instead of serving revenge cold, he was nothing but hugs and two-hundred-dollar pens and pervy gratitude and—

"Mom?" It was Timby.

He held up what he'd been reading, from Spencer's bag, a fancy magazine or catalog…It took me a second to even recognize it.

THE MINERVA PRIZE

From my *Looper Wash* days. It was a prize (now defunct) for graphic novelists. I'd been nominated for one in 2003 by Dan Clowes.

That year's Minerva Prize winner was going to be announced at a dinner at the Odeon. We were in the middle of production on *Looper Wash* and I intended to blow off the ceremony. But at the last minute, I grabbed the gang and walked over. We were horribly underdressed and seated at a good table. Across the expertly lit orchid centerpiece, the wife of the arts commissioner looked askance at our rowdiness and dirty jokes. (Ask anyone: being in production on a TV show turns you feral.) I didn't expect to win, and didn't. We each came back with a swag bag: POM Wonderful, a Murakami thumb drive, a mug with the Bear Stearns motto: Ahead of the Curve (!).

And that program.

"I wasn't invited to the ceremony, of course," Spencer was telling Timby. "But the next morning I fished a program out of the trash.

The other day I was doing some spring cleaning and came across it. I thought your mom might want it."

Something terrible was occurring to me...

"What?" asked Spencer.

...that program, the one Timby had in his hands. It had profiles of each nominee and their work...which meant *my* work, all twelve illustrations.

"Hey," I said to Timby, reaching across. "Gimme that."

He yanked it away. "Who are the Flood Girls?"

The Flood Girls

Eleanor Flood

The Flood Girls
Nominated
by
Daniel Clowes

I first met Eleanor Flood in 1995, back in the olden days of what we once called the San Diego Con (to differentiate it from Dallas Con, Sac Con, Leper Con), a few years before it was gentrified by Hollywood, and comics were still the main focus. Off in the indie/alternative/underground ghetto corner it was me, Peter Bagge, Joe Matt, the Hernandez brothers, Ivan Brunetti; the usual gang of idiots. We'd sit at tables with our art spread out, praying that Matt Groening would come along and buy something. We were strong believers in *noblesse oblige*.

For long stretches, nobody even glanced our way and the only time we got anyone was when the line for Todd McFarlane was so long that the occasional bearded man-child would shuffle a few steps off his path to deliver a disdainful glare or perhaps to use one of my originals as a coaster for his drink.

It was during a soul-numbing moment of career introspection such as this that an anomalous young woman emerged from behind the crowd. She had good posture and wore a dress (an actual dress, not a Troll Queen dress). She was apparently a fan of *Eightball* because she recognized the pages I was selling. "*Ghost World*! That's the cutest!" and "I can't believe you're selling *Ugly Girls,* it's super-cute." *Cute* wasn't a word I usually heard in relation to my art (*Ew* was number one, followed by *Why?*). I saw her turn to survey the now-endless McFarlane line. "I suppose I should feel sorry for them," she said. "What's the point in that?" I responded. "They don't even know they're sad." We discussed whether this gave us the right to hate them and agreed that it probably did. Then she picked up my whole portfolio and asked, "Would it be bad if I just bought *everything?*" I told her that would be fine.

She wrote me a check. ELEANOR FLOOD. NEW YORK, NY.

The next time I saw her was nine years later. I was in New York for something and promised my sister I'd go see my nephew who was answering phones for a production company. She said, "You know the show. *Looper Wash.* The short about girls on ponies that played before *Ice Age* and now it's a series on Fox?" I had no idea what she was talking about (thank God), so I just said, "What's the address?"

I went to a building in SoHo, which sounds impressive but surely was not, and walked up to the fourth floor. Apparently, everyone was in a screening down the hall because the place was deserted. In a corner office I saw a drawing board with a big mirror propped in front of it. That struck me as exactly the kind of ego-maniacal, solipsistic self-focus I so admire in myself, so I went over to explore further.

On the drawing board (along with viciously mean doodles of Fox executives, which instantly endeared this person to me) were colored-pencil illustrations. They were busy and "pretty," full of soft tints and delicate expressions, which aren't qualities I usually go for. But they were also disturbing, and not in the usual ironic Jughead-with-a-crack-pipe way. They were disturbingly sincere.

I heard a bubbly voice. "Dan Clowes!" It was Eleanor Flood. Turns out she was the animation director at *Looper Wash* and my nephew had told her I was coming. She pulled out the portfolio of my art that she'd bought years before.

"Do you want any of these back?" she said. "A lot of them are probably worth a fortune now. I feel bad. I could cry sometimes thinking of how little I paid for them."

I actually *had* cried thinking the same thing. I told her she could keep them.

She saw me looking at her drawings. "I know," she said. "Aren't those super-cute?"

Yes, they were, I said, studying them for an awkwardly long time. "The Minerva asked me to nominate," I said. "Do you think I could submit these?"

"But isn't that for graphic novelists?" she asked.

"Put these together and you've got a comic." Even back then, I couldn't bring myself to use the term *graphic novel*. She got what I meant.

"Oh," she said.

Unlike many stories about childhood, *The Flood Girls* feels immediate and present-tense urgent. Though it's dense with period detail, a nostalgia trip it is not. The vantage is frank and unsentimental. That Eleanor Flood is able to infuse these ominous, cryptic images with so much warmth is a rare trick, and I look forward to seeing more.

THE
FLOOD
GIRLS

Tess Tyler and Matthew Flood
Bemelmans Bar, 1967

Eleanor 4, Ivy 6 mos.

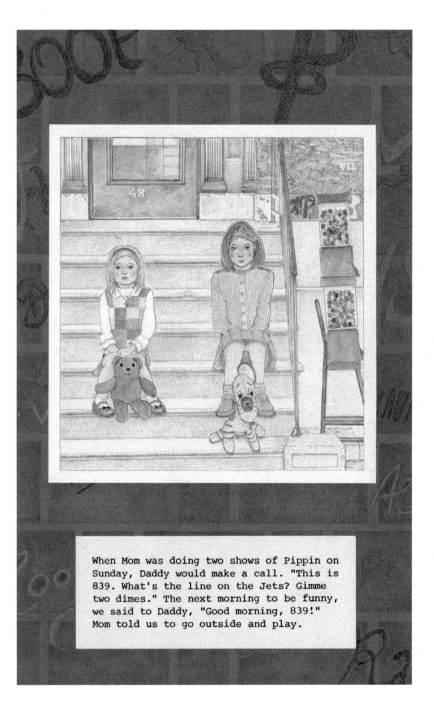

When Mom was doing two shows of Pippin on
Sunday, Daddy would make a call. "This is
839. What's the line on the Jets? Gimme
two dimes." The next morning to be funny,
we said to Daddy, "Good morning, 839!"
Mom told us to go outside and play.

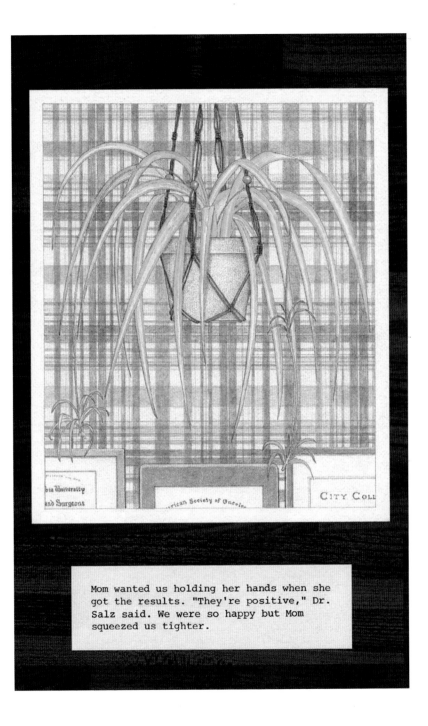

Mom wanted us holding her hands when she got the results. "They're positive," Dr. Salz said. We were so happy but Mom squeezed us tighter.

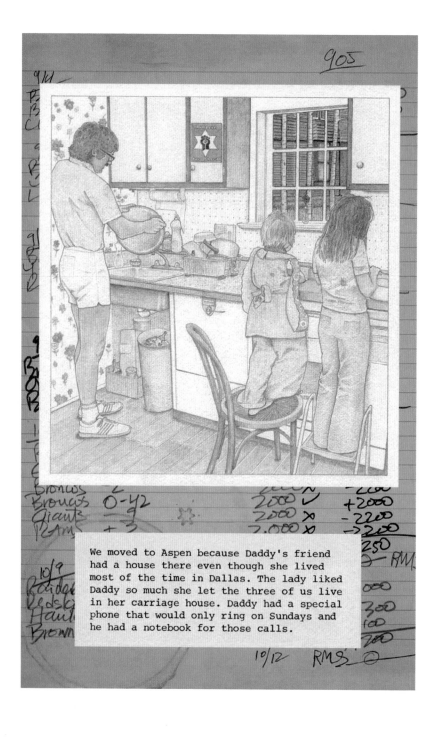

We moved to Aspen because Daddy's friend
had a house there even though she lived
most of the time in Dallas. The lady liked
Daddy so much she let the three of us live
in her carriage house. Daddy had a special
phone that would only ring on Sundays and
he had a notebook for those calls.

Daddy brought home a puppy he got for free outside of City Market. He named her Parsley because at City Market, parsley was always free.

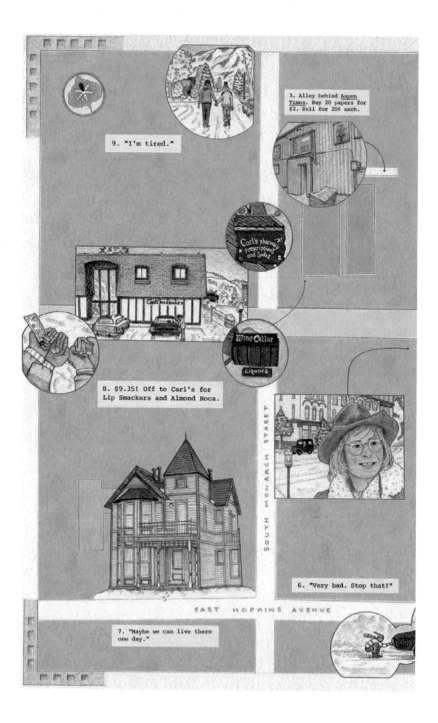

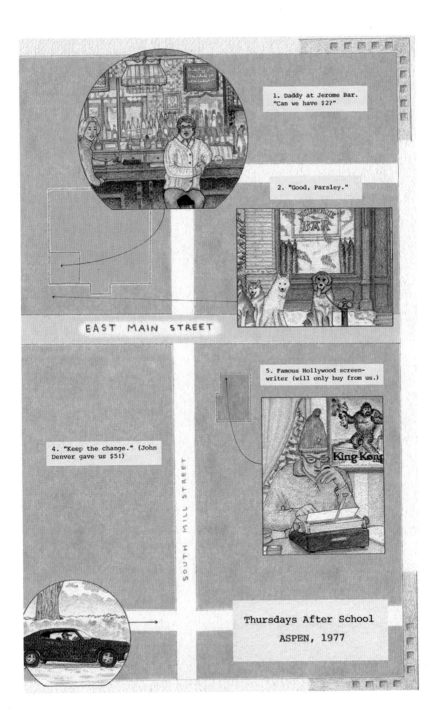

THE ASPEN TIMES

Vol. 96 * No. 23 * June 9, 1977 * Aspen, Colorado 81611 * 20 Cents * 3 Sections

Escaped kidnapper Bundy eludes

courtroom.

That library is separated from the courtroom itself by a partition about five feet high, with a door to it that is not locked.

Bundy was next seen by Casey
security
 cement
st the
line

'77 The Aspen Times Page 3-C

Ted Bundy was loose and school was cancelled so Daddy had to take us on his Tuesday morning errands. We had to wait in the car while he gave people envelopes or they gave him envelopes. "Don't open the door for anyone."

nder James Dumas stands in front
after Bundy's escape. He said no
d ever shown a "greater lack of
y jumped from the window at top

Theodore R. Bundy is escorted into the Pitikin County Courthouse in handcuffs the morning of his escape by Pitikin County Sheriff's Officers Pete Murphy, left, and Rick D Kralicek. Murphy is carrying Bundy's legal papers in the cardboard box. Bundy was brought to pre-trial hearings from the Garfield County Jail where he had been transferred because of fears about the security at the Pitikin County Jail.

In previous appearances, Bundy had wearing in this photograph was left made his jump to freedom. Some the ground near the spot wher replaced inside the courthouse Mark Lewy.

There was a racket in the kitchen, loud, even for Daddy coming home late. We got out of bed to see what it was. But then Daddy came out of his bedroom in his boxers rubbing his eyes. A bear was in the kitchen stealing our food! The police came and scared him away with a sandbag gun.

Every night after that, we'd hear the rattle of the front door knob. Then the side door. Then the back door.

Cracked Actor

"You never told me you had a sister," Timby said to me over the top of the catalog.

"I don't have a sister," I said.

There it was, finally: my lie, now a citizen of the world.

Before I fell asleep at night, I'd cycle through the various intonations in my head, preparing myself for this awful, inevitable moment.

I don't have a sister.

I *don't* have a sister.

I don't *have* a sister.

I don't have a *sister.*

Sometimes I'd say it out loud without realizing. Timby from the backseat: "What do you keep saying?" Me from the front: "Nothing."

Sometimes it would show on my face.

Joe: What are you thinking about?

Me: Nothing, why?

Joe: Your teeth are bared.

"But Tess Tyler was your mom," Timby said. "And Parsley was your dog and—"

"*The Flood Girls* represents two sides of me," I snapped. "It was an artistic experiment. That's all."

The French fries arrived, a crispy umber heap sprinkled with chopped fresh herbs.

"Whoa!" Timby said. "I call most of them!"

Could it be? Could I have just gotten away with the whole thing?

"Wait till you try the ketchup," I said, a tremor in my voice. "They make it themselves."

But Spencer...

Confusion had broken out across his face. His eyes were squinting. His brows were coming together. His mouth was opening. Words were coming out.

"But didn't I meet your sister?"

For clarity: I do have a sister. Her name is Ivy. I created *The Flood Girls* as a gift for her. Until Dan Clowes happened across those illustrations years ago, it had never occurred to me to turn them into a graphic novel.

Enter Joyce Primm, junior editor at Burton Hill, doing what junior editors did: troll obscure prize dinners for promising talent. Late twenties, rail-thin, pure confidence, Joyce cornered me in the Odeon ladies' room.

"Violet Parry gets all the credit for *Looper Wash*," she said. "It's time we right that wrong."

"Nice try," I said. "But Violet is a dear friend. No crime has been committed."

"I want more Eleanor Flood," Joyce said. "*The Flood Girls* begs to be expanded."

"This is highly flattering," I said. "But I'm no graphic novelist."

"Daniel Clowes thinks otherwise," she said. "So do I."

"I have no story to tell," I said.

She handed me her card. "Call me when you change your mind."

Then, years later, something terrible happened.

And I did have a story to tell.

I called up Joyce, by then executive editor of Burton Hill. She flew to Seattle.

We had drinks at the W Hotel. Joyce had on three-inch heels, peach pants, a floral crinkly silk shirt buttoned low, and a long gold chain. Her face was makeup-free and she wore her long hair in an effortless chignon.

Anytime I get into a one-on-one social situation, especially if there's something at stake, my anxiety spikes. I talk fast. I jump topics unexpectedly. I say shocking things. Right before I push it too far, I double back and expose a vulnerability. If I see you about to criticize me, I leap in and criticize myself. (One shrink labeled this The Trick. Halfway through our first session, he stopped me mid-yak. He said I was so afraid of rejection that I turned every interaction into a life-or-death charm offensive. That I was so unrelentingly verbal made me, in his opinion, untreatable. He handed me back my check and wished me luck.)

The best/worst thing about The Trick? People fall for it every time!

Over drinks, Joyce and I became instant buddies. Moscow

Mules became dinner, became "You've got to see this cute hat I bought." Upstairs in her room, Joyce gave me her cologne; I'd admired the scent but it could be bought only in Paris. I told her she dressed like a spring when she was really a summer; I wrote her a list of colors she needed to start wearing. She confessed to being on the verge of an affair with a married author. I told her I was the direct descendant of a U.S. president. I'm not speaking metaphorically when I say we tried on each other's shoes.

It was one in the morning before I remembered. "The book!"

"You may not know this yet," Joyce said, masterfully switching into editor mode. "But you're a writer. You think like a writer. Yes, I want those *Flood Girls* illustrations. But I want your words too. Is the book mostly words? Mostly pictures? I don't know. Every book has to invent itself. I'm giving you complete freedom. Use those illustrations. Just put what's in there..." She pointed to my head and said, "On the page."

I don't know if I got Joyce Primmed or if she got Eleanor Flooded. But I skipped out of there with a book deal.

"I did meet your sister," Spencer was saying, utterly flummoxed. "She was willowy. She always came by."

"Must have been someone else," I pronounced and sealed it with a smile.

Spencer looked like the guy in *Alien* before he started blurping up that white stuff. He checked his watch.

"Hi," he said to a passing waiter. "Would you mind terribly bringing us the check?"

"Now?" Timby said, having hardly made a dent in the heap of fries.

"We'll get a box for those," I said.

I don't *have* a sister.

I don't have a *sister.*

"French fries aren't good to go," said Timby.

"You two stay," Spencer said. "I have to find my way to the sculpture park for a meeting with my curator."

Thank God Spencer had no way of knowing we lived three blocks from the sculpture park, that it was where I brought Yo-Yo for his midday walk—

"We're going there too!" Timby erupted. "We can give you a ride."

I saw panic in Spencer's eyes.

"No, darling," I said to Timby. "Spencer's a busy man. He's not going to want to come home with us first and get the dog, and you know."

"I can show you my art!" Timby said to Spencer. "And then you can show me your art!"

Timby's voice had a plaintive little squeak to it.

Spencer = trapped animal.

Lying in bed this morning, I had set the bar laughably low: look people in the eye, get dressed, smile! It should have been a Sunday drive. Then that prankster Reality appeared in the pickup truck ahead of me and started tossing watermelons out the back. And it wasn't even one o'clock!

Today, at the very least, I'd fulfill my promise to Timby. I'd make it his day.

I looked at Spencer with what must have been desperation.

"Sure," he said. "I guess we could all go."

"Yay!" cried Timby

"I owe you one," I whispered to Spencer as we left the restaurant.

"It all evens out," he said tightly.

I flung open the front door with a flourish that said the hills were alive with the sound of music, when really I wanted a head start to make sure the toilets were flushed. On the off chance Spencer still admired me, I didn't want to queer it by him seeing our toilets full of pee.

Guess who didn't greet me at the door? Yo-Yo. He didn't even raise his chin off the rim of his bed. The most he could muster was to follow me around with watery, put-upon eyes.

"Would you look at this view?" I said, momentarily confused that I was Spencer seeing my apartment for the first time.

Spencer couldn't help but be pulled toward the floor-to-ceiling windows and our cartoonish panorama of Seattle: snowy Mount Rainier, Space Needle, Pacific Science Center arches, container ships of Elliott Bay.

"We were so nervous about the infamous Seattle weather that Joe said, 'Let's give ourselves half a chance of avoiding a murder-suicide and get a place with lots of light.'" I had to stop talking!

I popped into the bathroom, flushed (nice save!), and emerged babbling.

"This is where the magic happens!" I said, presenting Spencer the walk-in pantry I'd converted to my studio. "Or doesn't, depending on the day."

Spencer poked his head in. The space was barely big enough for my drawing table; the walls pinned floor to ceiling with a mad jam of photos, images torn from magazines, notes to myself, random trinkets. On the floor, waist-high stacks of the photography books I use for reference, and a glass jug that held the stubs of all the colored pencils I'd ever burned through.

"Thank God you're an artist," I said to Spencer. "Most people who sneak a peek think I'm batshit."

Spencer couldn't resist a closer look at my current project. I was working on a commission for the Telluride Film Festival, fiddling around with the idea of the knots in aspen trees looking like eyes. Or something. Scattered on the desk were strips of film, glass eyes I'd found at a curio shop, and an out-of-print book flagged for Herbert Bayer photographs.

"Imagine being you!" I said. "Seeing the inside of my car, apartment, and studio in the same day. It must feel like skipping first and second base and going straight to third!"

"If I'm making you nervous," Spencer said, "I can just go."

"Don't go!" I screeched, scaring even myself.

Joe's and Timby's breakfast dishes were still on the table, a diorama of half-eaten toast and half-finished orange juice.

"It's like the final day of Pompeii around here!"

"You and your sister," Spencer said quietly. "It's none of my business what happened. I'm not judging. You can stop."

"*Stop what?*"

"Why are you guys fighting?" Timby asked.

"How about you show me that art," Spencer said.

I hustled into Joe's office. For the first time since the shock of *The Flood Girls,* it was just me and me. My body knew it and involuntarily dropped into Joe's leather chair.

This. Shit!

The lethargy pressed down on me. My breathing slowed. I lowered my face into my spiderweb fingers.

Ivy. Whenever I think of her, the first image I always have, she's in profile, in her twenties, smiling, curious. She was born trusting and stayed that way, believed in people, saw the good in their stories, in their intentions, played along with how they wanted to be perceived. Her skin was so delicate you could see a blue vein running along her strong jaw. Her physical beauty was the first thing people noticed. She spoke quietly, drawing them into where they wanted to be, closer to her.

I wonder if she learned that from our mother, who could only whisper toward the end. Mom's friend Gigi would pick Ivy and me up every day after school and take us to the hospital. Each day, Mom's voice grew weaker.

Then one day, it was Daddy standing at the school gate.

I was nine. Ivy was five.

My memories of our mother's death (not the dying itself, but the days after) are a numb jumble dominated by my father's cluelessness and the flamboyant grief of show people.

Forty years later, though, the memories that cause my chest to curl in and ache are those of Ivy.

Within a week of her death, Mom's friends threw a celebration of her life. Broadway was dark on Mondays, so they borrowed the Minskoff, where Bette Midler was doing a one-woman show.

Daddy, Ivy, and I arrived at the theater and found ourselves receiving condolences in a random huddle in the center aisle. At the back of the stage, in the shadows, was the huge mechanical ape hand in which Bette Midler made her entrance.

The lights flickered. Father Kidney started up the steps to the mic. But the theater wasn't a quarter full.

"Shouldn't we wait for everyone?" I asked Daddy.

"It's a big theater," he said, and we took our seats.

I began to tremble. This was how her "tribe," as my mother called her theater friends, wanted her remembered? A priest speaking on a borrowed stage in front of another woman's props to an empty house?

My mother wasn't theirs to humiliate. She belonged to me. She was elegant and precise. She'd gone to boarding school in Switzerland and made us cheese soufflés in little ramekins and posed nude for a German photographer and filled our house with fresh flowers.

I turned to Ivy. "We're leaving."

"I want to see the show."

I yanked her away. We sat on velvet chairs in the lobby and fell asleep, awaking to the wail of bagpipes.

Daddy couldn't face sleeping in their bed so he'd been spending the nights on the couch. But it was the cat's couch. The morning after the memorial, the three of us were silently eating the food people had brought. (Weird stuff in unfamiliar casseroles: shepherd's pie with ground beef, not lamb; lasagna that tasted of cinnamon; macaroni and cheese with peas: all of it only compounding our dread of what the world would be like without Mom in it.) The cat hopped up on the couch, squatted over the spot where Daddy's head had been, and, staring straight at us, peed. It was completely evil and felt personal, as if Pumpkin were saying, *You think you have it bad now? Try this.*

I guess Daddy had to take his bottled fury and fear out on something, and better the cat than us. But still, I should have hurried Ivy out of there.

That afternoon, Gigi and another friend of Mom's, Alan, came over, and Daddy took Ivy and me to the park.

When we returned, Gigi and Alan were gone. The couch was gone. Pumpkin was gone. Everything of Mom's had been removed: the dresses in her closet, the sweaters and silk scarves folded in her drawers, the hats on the shelves, her jewelry, her makeup. Even her lingering smell had vanished.

In the hallway sat two boxes. One marked ELEANOR. One marked IVY.

The only thing Daddy kept were Tyler family heirlooms: a pair of antique derringers.

That night, while Daddy snored in his bed, I stared at those two boxes for hours. I finally picked them up, walked them to the incinerator chute, and tossed them in. (The scratch of sequins and beads against cardboard still haunts me.)

A week later, Daddy drove us to Colorado. He didn't tell us it would be one way. He'd met a woman from Dallas who had a second house in Aspen. We could live in the guesthouse in exchange for Daddy doing maintenance and small repairs. (In the '70s, Aspen was a funky former mining town with the best powder in the world, attracting mostly Texans. It was more cowboy hats and Wranglers than Mariah Carey and Gulfstream 550s.)

In New York, Daddy had installed sound systems for a living. His hope was to do that in Aspen, but something must have happened. I've since learned that many bookies started as gamblers who got in too deep and had to work off their debts.

The first time he left us alone was our first winter there. "You can take care of your sister?" Daddy had asked me. It was an odd question. He said we could sign for what we needed at Carl's Pharmacy. (Everything with Daddy is still a puzzle with missing

85

pieces. My best guess is that he drove to Vegas to lay off Super Bowl bets.)

He was gone nine days. Ivy and I lived by ourselves in the guesthouse. ("Come, let's away to prison. We two alone will sing like birds i' th' cage." That was the *Lear* speech Mom used to recite before bed.) It was January. When the school bus dropped us off, we'd hit Carl's, then slip into the little gingerbread house like thieves, the sun already behind Shadow Mountain. We'd turn on all the lights, start a fire, watch TV, and eat our haul of pharmacy Jolly Ranchers, Pringles, and whatever random piece of fruit sometimes appeared on top of a barrel by the back register.

A few days in, Ivy got sick and sicker. A 102 fever, wet cough, and earache that had her moaning. We didn't even have a pediatrician. If I called 911, the police would know we'd been left alone. We'd be taken away, most likely separated. I forged Daddy's signature on notes to school and nursed Ivy with whatever beckoned from the shelves at Carl's. Aspirin, VapoRub, Sucrets, throat spray, Benadryl, cough syrup—the what-might-have-beens still send shivers. I'd return home every day praying Ivy was alive.

She always was, and wanting to hear stories about what had happened at school. (Six she was. Being raised by a fourth-grader.) I didn't dare tell her the truth. I was a fat kid with red hair and freckles. New to town, having moved midyear from New York, I was tempting prey for the tough kids. As I walked on the path between classes, they'd push me into the pond. I wouldn't fight as they filled my backpack with heaps of fresh powder. Snowbaths, these wintry interludes were called.

But at home, in my afternoon reports to Ivy, I'd have the last word, mocking the bullies' appearances, ridiculing their names, belittling their intellects. "You're awful!" Ivy would say through her laughter, my audience of one.

But she knew I wasn't awful.

Once, years later, when we were in our twenties and walking up Madison Avenue, Ivy took my hand, just to hold. Such was our ease.

Despite everything that's happened between us, when I'm taken by surprise, the feeling I have of Ivy is one of tenderness: that day, taking my hand.

Now, with Ivy erased, I've become The Trick. I'm a grotesquerie going out into the world fetching observations and encounters to perform for someone who long ago left the building.

As I sat there at home, in Joe's office, a toxic, roiling mass bloomed in my stomach. Guilt, longing, regret: name it, it was in me, black, corroding me from within.

I couldn't help that being coldcocked with a reminder of Ivy triggered this wave of nausea and weakness. What I was feeling? It wasn't *me*. It was an isolated sensation that appeared in my stomach. It had edges. My job was to recognize it as an entity separate from myself.

Smell the soup. Cool the soup.

I'd rather be me right now. Ivy was off living a life of idiotic facades, laughable values—

I stopped myself.

I wasn't doing that. My business was my life. My life was an honorable one of self-generating abundance. I was healthy. Timby was healthy. Joe was healthy. I was loved. I'd made an impact as an artist. I had a graphic memoir to write. So what if I didn't get along with my sister?

I stood up, still a bit trembly, and started to leave, then stopped.

On Joe's desk. A telescope of some kind. Gray, the size of a demi-baguette, on crouching insect legs. It was aimed out the window.

How bizarre.

"I want to see!" It was Timby, followed by Spencer, his face covered in tiny flower stickers.

"Get away." I hip-checked Timby before he could get his hand on it.

"You're mean."

"Out, out." I herded them into the living room.

"Mom, can we use your computer to watch walking-stick videos?"

"I have to get going," Spencer said.

"One second." I shut the door.

I stepped behind Joe's desk, tucked my hands behind my back in reverse prayer, and lowered my face to the eyepiece.

Between the putty blur of foreground condos, a distant yacht leaped brightly into view. Black-hulled and sleek, just the prow peeked through in sharp focus.

I walked to the window. There it was, at a random dock at an industrial waterfront I never thought about but did pass on my way to Costco.

Hmm. A ship.

I stepped back, knocking over a date-tree stalk that was propped against the wall. Waist-high and edged with triangular spikes, sharp like shark teeth, a hundred twiny fronds dangled from the top like a prehistoric pom-pom.

Joe had brought it back from Turkey where he'd gone to do contracture-release surgeries. While there, he'd met a man who'd crossed the desert from Iraq with his cloudy-eyed father; they'd heard American doctors could make the blind see. As payment, they'd sawn off a branch from the family's date tree, heavy with fruit. Joe explained he wasn't that kind of doctor. They insisted Joe try a date anyway. The sweetness of the fruit might change his mind.

Joe lugged that stalk on four planes so he'd never forget those men. "*I* want to forget them!" I cried when Joe told me the wretched tale. "Get that thing out of here!" He'd brought the stalk to work only to have Ruthie chase it out too. It ended up here in the corner.

I returned to the big room and sat down at Joe's place at the table. I pushed aside the dishes.

"It's where they make clothes for H&M." Timby's voice, through the cracked door to his room.

"I can see why that would make you feel bad." Spencer's voice.

Click-click-click. Yo-Yo, standing there, dim and hopeful.

"Everything I say." Timby's little voice. "Piper acts like she knows more. I was telling her how I hate the Disney princesses —"

"You love the Disney princesses!" I shouted.

"I never liked them!" he shouted back.

"Halloween you went as Gaston, and Gaston loves Belle, so —"

Slam went Timby's door.

I lowered my forehead onto the table. It was much harder and colder than you'd think. I spread my arms out and up, just as Joe had done this morning. Not comfortable. Definitely not a position you'd find yourself in naturally. But what did it say? *I'm depressed. I'm alone. I'm hurting. I need help.*

I sat up. Yo-Yo cocked his head. His tail dared to wag.

"Go away."

"I know, right?" Timby said from his room. "I know, right?" Spencer answered. "I know, right?" Timby jumped in. "I know, right?" Spencer said on top of him. And on and on, until it was staccato and rapid-fire and I half expected a disco song to erupt, but instead it was giggles. God bless the gay and the young. Or the gay and the gay.

"Let's do this thang," I said, looking at Yo-Yo. "Who wants a walk?"

Having heard the magic word, Yo-Yo started barking.

"It's all true!" I said in my high-pitched Yo-Yo voice. "Let's go, Charlie Trotter. Let's go, Biscuit. Let's go, Yo-Yo-san. Let's go, Yoozy Von Boozy."

"His name is Yo-Yo," said Timby coldly, now standing there with Spencer.

"It's my tell," I said. "When I'm anxious, I make up nicknames for the dog."

"What do you have to be anxious about?" Timby asked.

"Things," I said.

Spencer held his tongue and we headed out to face the second half of the day.

"Okay, let's get this over with," I did or didn't say out loud as we walked down the steep incline, the autumn wind whipping through the corridor of apartment buildings. The Olympic Sculpture Park, once a contaminated industrial site and now an impeccably designed waterfront public space, hummed with activity.

A busload of children played hide-and-seek in a valley of rusty Richard Serras. Lovers lolled on quilts in the shadow of an enormous Calder, a pop of red amidst the cool blues and greens. A bicycle club rested at the Claes Oldenburg typewriter eraser, and squirted water into their mouths. Teens with Down syndrome, gripping handles on a rope line, hooted as they weaved through Louise Bourgeois's black marble eyes. Tourists snapped gag pictures of themselves holding the Space Needle in their palms. Sculptures everywhere, whimsical or baffling, challenging or just plain lovely.

Placed near all, discreet plaques etched with names of donors well known in Seattle and beyond: Gates, Allen, Wright, Shirley, Benaroya.

Taking in the joyful mix drawn together by a common enjoyment of art, I couldn't help but think: rich people, you gotta love 'em!

"I'll catch up with you," Spencer said and ran in the direction of the glass pavilion marking the park's entrance. If he didn't stop until he crossed into Canada, I wouldn't have blamed him.

Timby and I headed along the wide path that gently zigzagged down to the water.

"I was sorry to hear about Piper," I said. "You need to tell me these things. Not if you don't want to. But come on, we're buds."

Timby jammed his head into my side and I put my arm around his shoulder.

"Mom?" he said. "What's your favorite season?"

"I'll have to go with the obvious. Spring."

"Mine is winter," he stated proudly.

"Winter?" I said.

"Because of snow."

"When have you ever seen snow?"

"Remember that time we went to the Salish Lodge and Dad's patient who owns it got us that really big room and then we woke up and it was super-quiet and then you said, 'Open the curtain,' and it was snowing and then I ran outside and rolled around in my pajamas and then I caught snowflakes on my tongue and then Dad and I made a snowman that was full of leaves and then I thought a bee stung me but it was just ice inside my slipper?"

"Why don't we do that more often?" I said.

"Because you don't like being cold."

Oof. Instead of my accustomed rat-a-tat-tat, I paused to let myself feel the ache of the myriad ways I've disappointed Timby.

We walked quietly for a while.

"Mama?" Timby said. "Piper Veal called me a bad word."

"What did she call you?"

"Then I'm saying a bad word."

"Tell me the first letter."

"C," Timby's voice cracked.

"C!" I said. "A third-grader called you the C-word?"

"Yeah. Cow."

"Cow?"

"Why are you laughing?" he said.

"I'm sorry. It's not funny. It's shocking and rude."

"It means I'm fat," Timby said.

"Oh, sweetie, don't say that. I wouldn't have you any other way. Besides, soon you'll shoot up like a bean stalk."

"I hope it's really soon," he said.

"When I was your age, my father took me shopping and I had to buy my clothes in the Chunky section."

"Who called it that?"

"I don't know," I said. "Some awful store in Glenwood Springs. There was a section with a sign. 'Chunky.'"

"Poor Mama!"

Eight. Eight was the best age.

"That's the thing about hard times," I said. "Generally speaking, one survives."

Yo-Yo stuck his head into a boxwood and emerged with half a burrito. If there's one thing that dog has a talent for, it's sticking his head into a bush and coming out with 7-Eleven. He gobbled the burrito, foil and all.

"Mom!" Timby cried.

I reached into Yo-Yo's mouth, hooked out the drooly stub, and tossed it in the trash. Yo-Yo, on the verge of panic, fixed his attention on me.

"It's gone!" I presented my empty hands with a Vegas dealer clap, but it meant nothing. "Let's go, you stupid dog."

I yanked the leash. He yanked back. I nudged him with my foot.

"Don't kick him!" Timby cried.

"That's not kicking."

People hadn't stopped to watch, but they were certainly slowing down to judge.

We arrived at the bottom of the hill, looked both ways for cyclists, and crossed the bike path onto a lawn that rolled down to the water.

A square of grass had been staked off in CAUTION tape. Within, two framed panes of glass were mounted on poles at eye-level.

"Is something going in those?" Timby asked.

Like I had any idea.

A guy in painter's pants and T-shirt was crouched over something, his back to us. At his side was a black plastic cart piled with tools.

Suddenly, a spray of water arched over our heads and squirted the glass. The worker jumped out of the way.

It was Spencer, behind us, pointing a hose.

"You found me!" he said.

The glass on the left glistened with water pebbles. But the one on the right...

"It's coated in high-tech liquid repellent," Spencer explained. "Water bounces right off."

I ducked under the yellow tape and touched the glass. It was magically dry.

"When the Seattle Art Museum commissioned an outdoor piece," Spencer said, "I thought, *Yay, I get to play with rain.* I remembered you'd moved here, *et voilà.*"

"Me?"

Spencer led me by the hand. The workman held a level between his teeth as he affixed a plaque to a concrete stump.

"CAREERIST / ARTIST"
SPENCER MARTELL
American, b. 1977

If it was shock and delight Spencer was after, I certainly delivered. In one frame, the cedars beyond wobbled through water drops. In the other, the same view, bold and crisp.

"*Careerist* is the canvas covered with tears," I said, figuring it out. "It's distorted by emotion. *Artist* is the identical image freed from self-pity."

Spencer's hands flew up to his face in mock horror. "Could you make me sound any more maudlin and faggy?"

Timby gasped at the bad word.

"This is what an artist does!" Who was I even talking to? "Look around. There's everything to choose from. The vastness of the sky, the blues of the water. Ferries, sailboats, mountains, and everywhere you look, people. Timby, come here." I was apparently talking to him.

He instinctively took a step back.

"Have you ever seen such abundance?" I picked up my son so he was eye level with the frames. "But this is art, daring to put a frame around something, signing your name, and letting it speak for itself."

"Listen to your mother," Spencer said.

"At Cooper Union, I had to take History of Photography. Who's the guy who took the pictures of those sisters? In the seventies? Lined up like a Christmas card, year after year?"

"Nicholas Nixon," Spencer said. "The Brown sisters."

"Thank you! I was having a serious problem with photography in general. When we got to Nicholas Nixon, I said to my professor,

'That's so random. *I* could have taken those.' And he said, 'But you didn't. Nicholas Nixon did. And he put his name on it. That's what makes it art.'"

"And he did it over and over," Spencer said.

"He persisted!" I said. "And it became a body of work." I turned to Timby. "I don't mean to ruin the ending for you, sweet child, but life is one long headwind. To make any kind of impact requires self-will bordering on madness. The world will be hostile, it will be suspicious of your intent, it will misinterpret you, it will inject you with doubt, it will flatter you into self-sabotage. My God, I'm making it sound so glamorous and personal! What the world is, more than anything? It's indifferent."

"Say amen to that," Spencer said.

"But you have a vision. You put a frame around it. You sign your name *anyway*. That's the risk. That's the leap. That's the madness: thinking anyone's going to care."

"Mom, you're saying the same thing over and over."

"I'm embarrassing you, am I?"

"Stop."

To throw gas on the fire, I stuck my butt out, assumed my shake-your-booty crouch, and—

My eyes locked on something through the tearstained glass.

Perfectly framed: the yacht.

The dock was a ten-minute walk up the bike path.

"Spencer?" I said. "Can you watch Timby?"

"Shoot," he said. "I'm meeting my curator in the pavilion."

"Perfect," I said. "Timby knows my number."

"Mom!"

I handed Timby my purse. "Gum, makeup. It's all yours."

"Ooh." He hooked the purse smartly around his shoulder. "Go."

The yacht, the third largest in the world, belonged to the Russian oligarch Viktor Pasternak, who'd gotten stinking rich on natural gas. Last month, he'd gone snorkeling in Hawaii, where one hooker got jealous of a different hooker and threw a black sea urchin at Viktor's head. He'd covered his face in time but the poisonous spikes got stuck in his hand. When it began to swell, he took off for Seattle because he'd heard about The Guy.

"A sea urchin defense wound!" Joe remarked gleefully when he received the call.

Viktor lived by a credo he'd dubbed the "eight-minute rule." He'd calculated he was rich enough that he didn't have to do anything he didn't want for more than eight minutes. That included being in hospitals, which he mortally feared due to an overreaction to a recent Anderson Cooper piece on antibiotic-resistant staph infections. (Viktor kept saying Cooper Anderson, but Joe didn't correct him.) So Viktor converted the disco on his yacht into an operating room. He'd invited Joe to the yacht, presented him with the state-of-the-art setup, and announced it was where Joe would be removing the hooker-delivered sea urchin spikes. Joe, not being insane, balked.

Viktor persisted. His equipment had been installed under the supervision of Spain's Dr. Luis Rogoway, famous for operating on the knees of European soccer stars. Rogoway, a great friend, would fly in his nursing staff, gorgeous Spanish women, none shorter than six feet, to assist Joe.

Joe thought about it. Audacious, yes, but unethical? No law said you had to operate in a hospital. Joe had done a hundred procedures on dirt-floored dwellings in Haiti, India, Ethiopia. Insurance companies wanted you to do everything in a hospital; this guy was obscenely overpaying in cash. It was an out-of-body moment, one Joe still didn't quite understand, when he heard himself saying yes.

Viktor had another stipulation: Joe had to clear his schedule for the week-long recovery. That's why Joe had told his staff he was out of town.

As for why Joe didn't tell me? He knew I'd be a gusher of opinions, all negative, and who needs that the night before you're performing surgery in an unfamiliar disco? Joe made the decision to operate, donate the money to charity, and laugh with me later.

On the appointed day, Joe opened Viktor's hand, removed the sea urchin spikes, and repaired the tendon damage without incident. Before closing the hand, Joe wanted to zap any lingering bacteria. He instructed the Spanish nurse to turn on the UV light. Her English being less than *bueno,* she hit the wrong switch. A pound of glitter dumped onto the operating table and into Viktor's open hand. After fifteen minutes of recriminations, panicked discussion about the relative filth factor of Chinese glitter, and a torrent of cursing straight from the Tower of Babel (much of it from the patient himself), Joe was frog-marched off the yacht by Uzi-packing security.

For days he'd been trying to get in touch with Viktor but he'd been cut dead. Joe whiled away the week at Mariners games. (It was heading into October so they were in the playoffs.) He'd bought a high-powered telescope to monitor the comings and goings around the yacht, still ominously in port. A black sedan from the state's medical board had arrived at the pier this morning. The thought of it was so revolting it had rendered Joe face down at the breakfast table.

Was I insane?

Joe hadn't operated on a Russian oligarch in the disco of his yacht!

He wasn't assisted by a staff of perfect-ten Spanish nurses (where did I come up with that, a Robert Palmer video?), one of whom had accidentally glitter-bombed the surgery!

The medical board doesn't have a black sedan!

The Mariners have no chance of making the playoffs!

This witch was on tilt.

The yacht, I realized when I arrived at the dock, was no yacht at all but a banged-up squid boat. How did I know? A van from Renee Erickson's restaurant empire was parked at the pier. A tattooed chef (is there any other kind?) haggled with a fisherman over a sea creature the size of a toilet.

A fluorescent cloud of cyclists whizzed past and practically knocked me off my feet. I was standing in the middle of the bike path, clueless and let down, unmoored from space and time. Yo-Yo sighed.

"You and me both," I said to him.

Could Joe have been looking at something *behind* the boat? No, across a small channel there was only a row of corrugated metal buildings: a nautical-supply house, a marine-fuel station, and, beyond them, a Costco.

I sat on a guardrail. Yo-Yo placed his front legs on my lap and waited for a head scratch.

What I knew: Joe had told the girls in the office he was out of town for a week. Spencer's call today had placed Joe at the end of that stretch.

But as of this morning he was facedown on the breakfast table. He must be going somewhere each day without telling anyone. And at some point, he'd aimed a telescope at this exact spot...

This was ridiculous. I called Joe's cell.

He picked up after one ring. "Hey, babe."

"Joe." My calm voice belied my heart, which had broken loose in my chest. "Where are you?"

"At the office. Why?"

Yow. I realized I wasn't dreading a scene, I was itching for one. I was ready to jack this party up to eleven and start breaking some plates. The last thing I could have fathomed was that I'd be lied to with such calm, clarity, and conviction. (C-words! They're everywhere today!) I'd like to say such a thing had never happened to me, but I knew sickeningly well it had, eight years before, at the hands of my sister, Ivy. It's the last impression I have of her, the cool betrayal. But now Joe? If there was one thing in this world I thought I could count on, it was that Joe was no liar. But here he was, lying.

Yo-Yo pawed at my lap. I'd stopped scratching his head.

"Just thought I'd check in." I matched Joe's nonchalance and raised him a bored sigh.

"All's well?" he asked.

"'I myself am hell, nobody's here, only skunks,'" I said. "You know how it is."

"Do I ever," he said.

"I had to pick up Timby at school. It's a long story involving cheaply made clothing, Bangladeshi slaves, and an antagonist with the last name Veal."

This was better than a scene! It was so exotic, so uncharted; it was forging a new pathway, the two of us, liars. I actually felt closer to Joe in a kinky, thrilling way. Lying! The middle-aged sex?

"I'll fill you in tonight," I said.

"I'm stuck at a thing," he said. "I might be late."

For years I'd been cataloging traits of Joe's that annoyed me, things I'd be relieved to have out of my life should he ever decide to leave me. The Gratitude List, I called it.

1. When I get out of the shower and ask Joe to hand me a towel, he invariably hands me a damp one.

2. He has never once *offered* to walk Yo-Yo. He'll walk Yo-Yo, but only after making me play the harridan.

3. When we go out to restaurants, he puts leftover dinner rolls in his socks and brings them home so they won't go to waste.

4. Said dinner rolls get placed on his bedside table until he notices them a week later, at which point he hands me the wheat stones and asks me to "use them in something." (Thus the frequency of bread pudding. No wonder poor Timby is a chunkster.)

5. Every time we go to a movie and it starts twenty minutes late because of the previews, Joe goes nuts, showing me his watch and informing me and everyone else in the theater what time the movie was scheduled to begin.

6. When we run a fan to cool down a room, he insists it point into the room, not out, which just seems wrong.

7. He puts sriracha on everything I make. Even waffles.

My Gratitude List was self-protection. I started composing it the morning after Joe and I first said "I love you," at Dojo on St. Mark's Place. Bob Marley's *Legend* was playing in the background. (This was New York in the '90s; when *wasn't Legend* playing in the background?)

Joe was due at the hospital at 5:30 a.m. He'd showered and dressed quietly enough. But then he sat at the end of my bed, on my feet (!), and put on his shoes. Just so you don't take me for a complete scorekeeping bitch (which I am, but there's better evidence), Joe freely admits he's "essentially selfish." It's the single piece of insight he received the one time he went to a shrink. (Me, on the other hand, I've been to nine shrinks in twenty years and I'm still like, "Wait...what?") This selfishness, according to Joe's miracle shrink, was a response to being one of seven children. Every time a box of Quisp or Quake was unpacked from the grocery bag, kids descended on it in a feeding frenzy. Joe shared a room with three brothers. Control of the remote, a private place to read *Playboy,* everything a cage match to the death. The fault, of course, lay with the Catholic Church, which encourages lower-class families to reproduce like rodents and build up the Church's ranks, blah-blah.

Another item for the Gratitude List: no more Joe railing against religion.

In fact, that dinner at Dojo, it wasn't Rasta Bob singing "I wanna love you, every day and every night" that inspired Joe to declare the three words that sealed our fate; it was the following discussion of the New Testament:

Joe: It's doggerel, aggrandizing a moody egomaniac written by men who believed heaven was a hundred feet above their heads. Literally. So when Christ ascended, He didn't go higher than a seven-story building.

Me: Who cares?

Joe: The hours I wasted listening to that contradictory claptrap! The things I could have done with that time! I could have learned another language. Or leathercraft.

Me: I was brought up Catholic too, you know. When I was seven, they were teaching us about the loaves and the fishes. I raised my hand and said, "That couldn't really happen." Sister Bridget, not happy, responded, "Faith requires the mind of a child." I said, "But I am a child." She replied, "A *younger* child." I thought, What a load of malarkey, and never looked back.

Joe: So you just turned atheist? Wasn't it a struggle?

Me: "Let's not and say we did" is my attitude.

Joe: I love you.

Me [I knew it was a blurt that didn't count. But still, you gotta jump on these things.]: I love you too, Joe.

I'd officially fallen in love the week before, in the Adirondacks, and was just waiting for him to say it first. Violet Parry, the creator of *Looper Wash,* had rented a lake house and invited the animators and their significant others for a bonding weekend. (I'd only just met Joe, so new work friends + new guy = doubly scary.) It was July 4th. Rumor had it if we hiked to the ridge we could watch the fireworks from the town on the other side. Only after evening fell and we were getting ready to go did we discover that none of the cabin's dozen flashlights worked. We groused and resigned ourselves to a boozy night on the porch. Joe didn't come outside. I found him alone at the kitchen counter. He'd disassembled the flashlights and laid them out like surgical instruments. He'd swapped bulbs, scrubbed off crusted battery ooze, and was folding tinfoil into small squares. So peacefully absorbed, so competent, so dear. (That was the moment.) I'm not kidding, within thirty minutes Joe had ten of those flashlights working. As we headed up the forest path, Violet pointed to Joe and mouthed, *Keep him.*

Had I lost him? Might there be someone else?

Yo-Yo's eyes were closed and his face was raised to the sun. Come to think of it, he *was* pretty useless. Thanks a lot, Joe. You left me for another woman and turned me against my dog. If Jerry Garcia were alive, he could sing a song about it.

The fisherman helped the tattooed chef load the squid into an ice chest. I caught them looking at me. Had they been talking about me? I gave them a nod. They carried on with their business.

I revisited my Gratitude List. Oh, another one! Joe reads in bed long after I go to sleep. No amount of passive-aggressive tossing and turning on my part, nor looking at the clock, nor dramatically putting a pillow over my head will make him turn off the light. When he finally does, he'll sometimes rest his book on me. And these aren't slim volumes of poetry. They're Winston Churchill biographies, and Winston Churchill lived a very full life.

The van door slammed shut. The fisherman was gone. The chef came around the side. Our eyes caught. I held his gaze. He held mine. It's not that I wanted to get anything going with this guy, but it was too weird...   ·

And then he was walking toward me with an intrigued half smile.

I don't put my hair in a clip for one day and this happens? A hot chef, knowing he's got a squid in the back of his van, boldly crosses a parking lot to start up a conversation with a middle-aged woman?

This brave new world could not have come at a better time.

"I have to ask," he said.

"I have to answer."

"What kind of dog is this?"

I was as desirable as a hedge. That's what happens when you lose your sex drive. I can put on Belgian dresses, wear my hair down, and flirt garishly, but when it came to real currency, sexual currency, I had none.

This morning when Joe said of Yo-Yo, "I know what he's getting out of *us*, I just don't know what we're getting out of *him*," he wasn't only talking about the dog.

I offered the chef the leash.

"He's a mutt," I said. "Want him?"

"Wow," he said. "No, but thanks. He sure is cute!"

With that, my Gentleman Caller disappeared into the ether.

It's not like I don't come with my own grab bag of flaws. Although Joe is far too superior to catalog his grievances toward me, they might include:

1. Once I ate a bagel on the toilet.

2. I use too much floss.

3. I floss in bed.

4. I take the dog into the shower with me to wash him.

5. I take my first bite of popcorn at the movies by touching my tongue to the top of the popcorn and eating what sticks. But Joe always says he doesn't want popcorn because it's too salty, so it's mine and can't I eat it the way I want?

6. I toss Milk Duds into the popcorn.

7. Actually, I bite the Milk Duds into four pieces and spit them back into the popcorn so they're smaller, giving me a better popcorn-to-Milk-Dud ratio. Yes, they're covered in saliva, but it's my saliva. Though I can see how, to someone reaching into the popcorn he said he wasn't going to eat, it could be an issue.

Joe wouldn't say this because he's a gentleman, but I will: I'm looking worse by the day. I'm all jowly. My back is dry. I have a bush the size of a dinner plate. My core strength is nonexistent. Menopause means your metabolism skids to a stop and you lose 30 percent of your muscle mass. In other words, the self-discipline to watch my weight, which I never had to begin with, I now need more of. Really, I'm hanging by a thread. Sure, Joe had spent breakfast with his face down on the table but at least he was still in the same room with me.

Yo-Yo, bored with the hot sun, let out a snorty yawn.

Come on, Gratitude List, work your magic! I haven't nursed you all these years for nothing! The whole idea was when Joe finally hit the eject button, *I'd* feel free too. Kind of like that first shower after getting my hair chopped off, or those first steps in a new pair of cushiony running shoes, or seeing the world through new, stronger prescription lenses...

Could this be happening? Could the elixir I'd been squirreling away for decades have lost its fizz?

Was it me? Was it Joe? Was it the passage of time? Was I too tired to care? Earlier this year, I'd told a mother at school I'd been married fifteen years. She asked, "What's the secret to a long marriage?" I thought for a second, then answered, "Staying married."

Was it happiness I'd found in my long marriage? Or capitulation? Or is that all happiness is, capitulation?

The story of our marriage was in frames all over our apartment: Joe and I riding to the Emmys in the back of a limo. Me surprising Joe during a medical conference in Chicago and having someone take our picture in front of Cy Twombly's peonies. (Moments later, Joe asked me to marry him in front of the Bean with a ring he'd grabbed at the museum gift shop.) Our wedding in Violet Parry's backyard in Martha's Vineyard. Giving birth to Timby at home on Thanksgiving Day, the TV on in the background, the cast of *Sunday in the Park with George* performing during the Macy's parade. *Sunday, by the blue, purple, yellow, red water.* Joe opening the Wallace Surgery Center. Timby's first day of kindergarten.

But standing there in the weak October sun, a different story of our marriage presented itself. It was as if all those years, Joe and I had been followed by a photographer snapping pictures of us unawares...

Joe and me reading quietly in bed, Timby playing Legos at our feet.

Me looking out the window, seeing Joe and Timby below, walking home from the Science Center.

Me standing on the Galer Street lawn in the drizzle, early for pickup.

Yo-Yo snoring in the living room, so loud none of us could sleep.

The three of us sitting on the curb outside Portage Bay waiting for them to call our name for brunch.

That was happiness. Not the framed greatest hits, but the moments between. At the time, I hadn't pegged them as being particularly happy. But now, looking back at those phantom snapshots, I'm struck by my calm, my ease, the evident comfort with my life.

I'm happy in retrospect.

Oh, Joe, take me back and I promise I'll make love to you twice a week and never eat a bagel on the toilet again. I'll appreciate the quiet moments and—

Hey! Could it be? Alonzo! Walking on a pedestrian overpass spanning Elliott Avenue.

I watched him go down the stairs and head into the Costco parking lot.

This was perfect. I needed to apologize for calling him "my poet."

Alonzo had changed into jeans and a red polo shirt, but he was unmistakable from afar with his sturdy frame and regal carriage.

"Let's go!" I said to Yo-Yo, who jumped so vigorously out of his sleep I feared we both might tear muscles.

Cars were few on the edge of the Costco parking lot. Yo-Yo's friskiness toggled to despair as I tied him to an empty shopping-cart rack and sliced the air with my index finger. "You. Stay."

Alonzo's mop top bobbed over the parked cars in the distance and stopped at a rack filled with pony packs of marigolds. Alonzo took in the unremarkable sight and threw his head back with a jolly laugh. Poets. I needed to be more like them.

Alonzo spotted something on the ground—I couldn't see what—and leaned over to pick it up. He then disappeared into the shadowy maw of Costco.

This was my Costco, and it wasn't like I hadn't lost Timby in here more than once, so I'd perfected the art of finding moving targets. My secret? To canvass the place like I was drawing that house with the X through it without lifting my pencil.

I entered and jogged along the left wall, checking the aisles to my right. When I reached the top left corner, I crossed through wine and hung a left, which landed me in toilet paper. Still no Alonzo.

*

Last time I was here was a year ago. After an hour spent filling my cart so high it handled like a bumper car and required an arm across the top so everything wouldn't slide off, I made my way to the checkout line. A wave of misanthropy swept over me. Why did that lady need a whole drum of Red Vines? What would someone even do with a hundred combs? Did that fatso really need a laminator all to herself? Couldn't she just go to Kinko's? Or that guy, what was he doing with six gallon jugs of generic scotch? And why must they all wear shorts?

Thank God I wasn't one of them! Me with my case of highly rated New Zealand sauvignon blanc, my pound of fresh pineapple spears, my salt-and-pepper pistachios, my twelve-pack of dental floss. *My* items painted a clear picture of my sophistication…my superior taste…my sparkling intelligence…

I abandoned my cart in the checkout line and walked out empty-handed. I felt bad for the person who had to return my stuff to the proper shelves. I felt worse when I realized it was probably cheaper for Costco to just throw it all away.

I crossed through produce. Impossibly cheap! Good color! Firm to the touch! What's the catch? Too many seeds. As good as it all looks on the outside, take it home and it's filled with a freakish number of seeds. English cucumbers: dense with flat leathery seeds. Lemons: you dull your knife on all the seeds. Cherry tomatoes: jammed with tiny, slimy seeds. Not that I'd ever buy chicken at Costco, but if I did, I could imagine slicing it open and seeds pouring out.

A mob of Seahawks fans blocked the way to the bakery. Racks of cupcakes were being rolled out, a dozen to a shrink-wrapped sheet, each frosted blue with a green *12*. Across the aisle, a bigger mob swarming cupcakes decorated with Pope hats, also with the number *12*. The only thing you need to know about Seattle? Nobody was offended.

I arrived at the gauntlet of food-sample people. They stuck to their script without deviation and avoided eye contact, America's version of the Buckingham Palace guards. If the Buckingham Palace guards had terrible posture and filled you with existential dread.

"Jack cheese," said a woman. "In four zesty flavors. Stock up for the holidays."

"Breaded steak fish," a voice droned. "Fresh from Alaska and a perfect option for a healthy nutritious dinner. Try it tonight. Breaded steak fish..."

My attention snagged on the slight Southern accent. My head jerked back. My body turned.

There he was, in a blue apron and shower cap, manning a little counter. My poet, with a marigold in the buttonhole of his polo shirt.

"Fresh from Alaska and a perfect option for a healthy nutritious dinner. Try it tonight."

I was jolted by the mash-up of high and low: the red plastic tray, damp and smelling of industrial dishwasher—his encyclopedic knowledge of the lives of the poets—the toaster-oven door stained brown with grease—

"Eleanor?"

"Alonzo!" I opened my arms for a hug.

He looked down: he couldn't step off his mat.

"What's this?" I said, picking up a little sample cup.

"Breaded steak fish."

"I've heard it's fresh from Alaska and perfect for a nutritious dinner."

"A perfect *option* for a *healthy* nutritious dinner," Alonzo corrected.

The whole exchange had an easy grace.

"Don't mind if I do." I dropped the morsel of fish on my tongue. Not my favorite.

Alonzo handed me a napkin and pointed to a trash can across the aisle. When I turned back, a man was standing at Alonzo's station, kicking the tires, so to speak, of free food.

"What's steak fish?" he asked.

"Tilapia," Alonzo answered.

"Tilapia?" the man said with suspicion.

"It's a sustainable, farm-grown replacement for pollack."

"Never heard of that either."

"It has the texture of steak," Alonzo offered.

The man took a bite. *"This?"*

"I think it tastes fabulous!" I said. "I'll take five cartons."

The wary customer shook his head as I grabbed my stack.

"See you next week?" I said to Alonzo.

"Same Bat Time."

"Oh," I said. "What's our next poem?"

"'At the Fishhouses,' by Elizabeth Bishop."

"But of course," I said.

Sometimes victory knocks on your window even though you never sent out an invitation. This is what today was supposed to be about! I had been present. I had been kind. I had radiated happiness. True, I'd completely forgotten to apologize to Alonzo. But I did turn what might have been an awkward situation into a respect-filled exchange bobbing with wit and sophistication. Chalk one up for me, leaving the world a better place than I'd found it.

But first, what to do with this goddamned steak fish? I made sure nobody was looking, nestled all five boxes in a bin of loose T-shirts, and got the hell out.

I stepped outside and got smacked by the sun. Yikes, I'd been gone forty-five minutes. Spencer hadn't called, which I considered a minor miracle. This middle-aged body would have to do the last thing anyone wanted to see: run back to the sculpture park.

"Wait!" It was Alonzo charging out, tugging at his blue apron as if being attacked by bees.

"Alonzo?"

He finally freed himself from the apron and whipped it to the ground. He crouched for a moment, hands on quads. This was no athlete either.

"I can't do it. The degradation, the dehumanization, the perversion of the English language." He pulled out a pack of American Spirits, tapped out a cigarette, and lit it with a mini Bic.

To my enormous credit, I didn't spend the next five minutes haranguing him for being a filthy, self-destructive smoker.

"It was that look on your face," he said after the first drag.

"My face was beatific and serene...wasn't it?"

"That made it worse. Seeing how hard you were working just to look me in the eye."

"I swear," I said. "I can't win for losing."

"I'm not sure that's what that means." Cigarette in his mouth, Alonzo picked up his apron, balled it up, and dropkicked it into a nearby dumpster.

"Oh, Alonzo," I said.

A motorized *zzzt* approached, followed by a slurring, high-pitched voice. "You don't want to do that."

It was a guy in a wheelchair with a tall safety flag. He wore a Costco name tag. JIMMY. His ear was frozen to his shoulder and his good arm worked a joystick.

"That's a twenty-five-dollar deposit on that apron," Jimmy said, scooting into Alonzo's personal space.

Alonzo kept smoking and listened with an air of amused detachment.

"I seen a lot of people flip out and quit," Jimmy continued. "Usually they throw their apron in the bin over there. Don't return it, and they deduct it from your last paycheck."

"Thank you," Alonzo said. "But I honestly don't give a rat's ass."

"Hey," I said. "You're a poet. Talk like one."

"They empty that trash at twelve, three, and six," Jimmy said. "I seen a lot of folks have second thoughts, come back but it's gone."

"I stand on my little mat flogging my fish story. Fresh from Alaska! On the box there's an icy, roaring stream jumping with sassy fish. Really, it's antibiotic-pumped tilapia farmed in Vietnam that maybe makes a *stopover* in Alaska. But hey, the price is right! Americans. You can see it in their walk. If they find something cheap, it puts a disgusting little bounce in their step."

"Okay!" I said.

"And yet, it genuinely pains me when people like you spit out my samples."

"I didn't spit it out!"

"I saw you," he said. "Yesterday was worse. Yesterday they gave me ostrich jerky."

"That was you?" Jimmy said, his chair leaping back with a *zzzt*.

"I didn't kill the ostriches. I didn't hang them up to dry and hack them into strips! I just handed it out. I'm a poet!"

"Do you mind if we do this in the shade?" asked Jimmy. He put his chair in reverse and *zzzt*'d backward.

"Do what in the shade?" I watched him recede farther away from where I needed to be, and yesterday: the sculpture park.

"Our talk!" Jimmy shouted from under the eave of Costco.

"We're not having a talk!" I said.

Alonzo lowered himself onto the curb, a three-step process accompanied by a fair amount of grunting.

"No, don't sit down!" I said. "Ugh! I'm telling you, I don't know whether to shit or go blind."

"Shit," Alonzo said. "It's hardly Sophie's choice."

He was now cradling his head in his hands. "Costco's the only insurance that pays for in vitro. My wife's going to kill me. But nothing is worth another hour of that place."

"Come on, Alonzo." I patted his back. "All work has dignity."

"She's right!" called Jimmy from the shade.

"Not that work!" Alonzo shouted back. He turned to me. A puzzled look befell his face. "Wait. What happened to your steak fish?"

"Right. Uh. It was delicious, but my son is with a stranger who expected me back an hour ago and the line was really long and—"

Jimmy motored over. "Where did you leave it? I'm not going to turn you in. It's just, it could thaw."

"In a basket of T-shirts."

"Oooh," Jimmy said. "You better show me."

"Yeah," Alonzo said. "Show him."

"No." I reached through my legs, pulled up the back hem of my dress, and tied it in a three-way knot. Looking like Gandhi from the waist down, I climbed the rungs of the dumpster.

"My life," I said, "is with my son, who I need to get back to before someone calls Child Services."

I snatched the apron and tossed it at Alonzo's chest. He let it bounce off.

"*Your* life," I said to Alonzo, hopping down, "is in that Costco." I tied the apron around his neck.

"Jimmy?" I said.

"Yes, ma'am!"

"Your life is escorting Alonzo back to his steak fish station."

"Can do."

"I'm a poet," Alonzo said. "I'm writing a novel. It's called *Marigold, My Marigold*. When I came to work, I passed a rack of marigolds. As I did, one broke off. This one. It was a sign. Today is the day my novel comes first."

"Alonzo," I said. "Quit tomorrow. I don't care. Just talk it over with your wife."

I aimed him in the direction of Costco.

"Go back to your darkling plain," I said, giving him a helpful shove. "Everything will be fine."

"My what?" Alonzo asked, turning back.

"Your little standing mat. Your darkling plain...pretend I never said it."

I'd love to tell you I jogged the half mile back to the museum at a measured and steady pace. Really, I sprinted with boobs flapping, R. Crumb calves wobbling, throat burning, blister on the inside of my right heel forming. And stopped after a hundred feet.

My phone vibrated in my pocket. Spencer must have waterboarded my number out of the recesses of Timby's mind.

"Yes, hello?"

"Am I speaking with Eleanor Flood?"

I took my phone away from my ear.

JOYCE PRIMM.

"Joyce, hi! I've been meaning to call!"

"This is Camryn Karis-Sconyers," the voice said. "I'm an editor at Burton Hill."

Whatever was about to happen, I had the strongest premonition I shouldn't hear it standing up.

I'd arrived at a small fishing pier. A Native American in a jean jacket sat on a bench with a portable radio. At his feet was a bucket filled with bloody gunk. BAIT 4 SALE. He nodded at the empty spot beside him. I sat down.

"Nice to meet you," I said to Ms. Karis-Sconyers.

"I'm calling because we're moving our offices downtown. I've been going through our files and found one for *The Flood Girls*. I'm wondering what you'd like us to do with it."

"Oh. Joyce will know."

"Joyce?"

"Joyce Primm," I said. "My editor. Let me speak with her."

"Um, Joyce Primm isn't with Burton Hill anymore."

So *that's* why Joyce had been calling, to tell me she was going to another publisher.

"Where did she land?" I asked.

"At a cheese shop in Nyack."

"Oh."

"I heard it's a really good cheese shop," Camryn offered.

So it hadn't been Joyce Primm calling. My phone just *thought* so because I'd entered Burton Hill's main number in my address book.

What a singular sensation, to have the facts of my career unraveling and raveling back up all at the same time.

"And, so, my book?" I asked.

"*The Flood Girls*?" she said. "It was kind of due eight years ago?"*

"Are you my new editor?"

"I edit YA."

"YA graphic novels? I'm sorry. I'm confused."

"We're not doing a lot of graphic novels anymore," Camryn said. "They were big ten years ago but we got burned by a few. You know, Joyce and her cheese shop."

"So you're saying my book is canceled?" I said. "You're just going to eat my advance?"

"I suppose we could sue you?" she said helpfully.

"That's okay."

---

* Did I say it was a *little* late? I guess it's eight years late. But I did say I was bad with dates. And numbers. And names. Although Camryn Karis-Sconyers is one I won't soon forget.

"I feel bad," Camryn said. "Maybe this is a conversation you should be having with your agent. Who's your agent?"

"Sheridan Smith," I said.

"Right."

"What?"

"Someone said she's a homeopath in Colorado."

"She is?"

"Publishing," Camryn said. "You might have heard. We've been going through a rough patch."

"Gee."

"You can still write your book," she said sweetly. "It probably just won't be for us. Oh!" She'd almost forgotten. "This file. I'm not sure if you want us to send it to you. Looks like contracts, correspondence, a Christmas card you drew for Joyce where instead of reindeer it's the *Looper Wash* ponies and instead of Santa it's that guy with the thing whose name I can't remember—"

I hung up and dropped my phone into the bait bucket.

I sensed a strong gaze. The Native American.

"Bad call?" he said.

"Bad call," I said, and walked away.

My oxfords crunched up the sculpture garden path toward the glass pavilion. My body was numb and made of feathers. People and sculptures grew denser until I was in thick with picnickers packing up, mothers chasing toddlers, tourists posing, the spindly legs of the red Calder spaceship teetering.

Oof. I was on the grass. I'd tripped on an outdoor light.

"I need help."

It was a story Joe once told. He was in Indianapolis for the NFL Combine and he'd gotten food poisoning. He'd spent all night on the tile floor of his hotel bathroom burning with fever. Vomit, sweat, diarrhea: name an orifice, there was something coming out of it. He found himself moaning, "I need help. Someone help me." As a doctor, Joe knew he didn't need help. His body simply had a bug and the quicker he expelled it, the better. But he found himself "made better in another way" by the act of repeating those words. "I need help. Somebody help me." He said them over and over until he started laughing. The next morning at breakfast he overheard people at the buffet. "Did you hear that poor fucker last night? I hope somebody helped him."

I hated that story. Joe was my Competent Traveler. He wasn't the one who laughed naked on the shower floor of a Holiday Inn Express. He didn't cry out helplessly to no one.

I'd forced myself to forget the whole episode. Until now.

I picked myself up off the grass. I sprinted the rest of the way, a bead of red running down my shin.

The glass of the pavilion was pure reflection. Orange the color of the birch leaves. Flat-bottomed clouds skipped across the sky. In a patch of inky ocean, I could make out Spencer standing with his back to me.

A sign: CLOSED FOR INSTALLATION. The door was propped open.

Spencer conferred with a gaggle of art types, at their feet a patchwork of furniture pads. Men in blue rubber gloves. The guy from before, still with the level in his teeth. An older woman with wild gray hair and harlequin-patterned tights spoke with her hands. Spencer noticed me over his shoulder. He shot me a *very* annoyed look.

Annoyance! How quaint!

I spotted Timby in the corner, legs folded impossibly underneath him, examining with quiet concentration the contents of my purse.

Timby with his pinch pots and darling belly and paper airplanes and backward *Y*s and his love of winter and carbs and walking sticks and his scavenging for clues to help him better understand the screwy adult world. Timby, it's not your fault my mother died when I was your age. You don't know that all the time you have with me from now on is a gift. It's not your fault I can't absorb that lesson myself. That I'm cobbled together from broken promises of jigsaw puzzles never started and pot-holder kits unopened. That's why Timby reads Archie! It's a steady group of characters behaving predictably. It's a world with the guarantee of small-scale problems. How do I break it to you that people aren't predictable? That life is confounding and sadistic in its cruelty? That when things go your way, it never makes you as happy as you'd expected, but when things go against you, it's a cold-water jolt, an unshakable outrage that dogs you forever. But I can be steady. I will show you kindness and bring you snow—

"Mom?" In Timby's hand was the ring of keys with the lanyard of baby blocks.

D-E-L-P-H-I-N-E.

From school! The ones I'd stolen. And completely forgotten about.

I darted toward him.

In my side vision, horror on the faces of Spencer, the installers, and the hip older woman, their mouths trying to warn me off something.

But I needed to get that awful name out of Timby's hand.

I raised my chin just in time to see a flat piece of metal with layers of green enamel, mottled like mold, across my field of vision.

Clunk.

The last thing I heard before I sank to the floor was Timby's voice.

"What are you doing with Delphine's mom's keys?"

Troubled Troubadour

Long before Eleanor met Bucky, she'd heard the stories.

Barnaby Fanning was the lone offspring of a marriage between two of New Orleans' finest families. Growing up in a Garden District mansion so iconic it was a stop on all the tours, the future heir to sugar and cotton fortunes both, his adolescence spent at debutante balls during the season and trips abroad during the summer: it was the stuff of true Southern gentlemen.

But Bucky always refused the first table at a restaurant. He carried a pocket calculator so he could tip a strict twelve percent. When his father nudged him out of the nest after graduating Vanderbilt (straight Cs), Bucky fluttered only as far as the carriage house because no other address would suit. He sported head-to-toe Prada bought on quarterly pilgrimages to Neiman Marcus in Dallas, paid for by Granny Charbonneau. At the slightest perceived insult, Bucky would fly into rages, becoming so red-faced and spitty in the process that even those on the receiving end of his invective grew concerned for his health. During the holidays, Bucky would stand over the trash and drop in Christmas cards unopened while keeping mental score of who'd sent them. He never accepted a dinner invitation without first asking who else would be there. Bucky Fanning had never been known to write a thank-you note.

There was a girl once, from an equally prominent family. A joining of the two would be the social equivalent of unifying the heavyweight title. Bucky would fritter away hours on the veranda dreaming of their wedding and life together. The girl was five years his junior; Bucky was at Tulane Law when she went away to Bard. The girl's first Thanksgiving back, Bucky arranged a party at Granny Charbonneau's, a proposal party. A hundred local eminences were in attendance, a videographer on hand to capture the moment. But the girl, a bit fuzzy on her status with Bucky, entered on the arm of her boyfriend, a film major, last name Geisler. Not German Catholic. It was widely appreciated that Bucky would never recover from the public humiliation. Indeed, he dropped out of Tulane.

Bucky now spent his days at the Williams Research Center in the French Quarter toiling away on a sprawling history of the Charbonneau family. He worked in the light-filled second-floor library in the mornings and walked to lunch at Arnaud's or Gala-toire's, the only places that would allow him to dine with his beloved Pomeranian, Mary Marge, perched on his lap.

In addition to his writing and seats on local charity boards, Bucky attended to the Court of Khaos. Khaos was arguably New Orleans' most elite social club, or "krewe." Bucky's father had been king of Khaos, his mother queen. Bucky had been a page in every court. When he aged out, he was elected captain. King might appear to outrank captain, but Bucky was quick to point out that king was ceremonial whereas captain wielded the real power: over membership, court assignments, invitations, float design, charita-ble disbursements, etc. During the season, August through Febru-ary, the court-related parties averaged five per week, climaxing in Mardi Gras, when the various krewes rolled through the French Quarter on floats, tossing beads and doubloons to the public before disappearing behind closed doors where that year's debutantes officially "came out" at lavish balls. Hierarchy, secrecy, exclusivity;

pageantry, privilege, tradition: the Court of Khaos was Bucky's unified field theory.

At times, Bucky's fervor for the debutante balls resembled that of a wedding-planner character from an '80s romantic comedy, a fey id gone wild. But New Orleans cossetted their eccentrics. The Skoogs had a grandfather who believed the Civil War was still being fought and indulged him with daily dispatches of Confederate successes. One of the Nissley girls spent second grade dressed as the Little Tramp. That the Fannings' eminently eligible son haunted the debutante scene but never seemed to risk romance, preferring instead to hover on the sidelines sneering at certain maladroit dancers and settling scores through seating charts, that was no different.

"I love this guy!" Eleanor said to Lester, looking up from her light box at the *Looper Wash* offices.

"He's really quite wonderful," Lester said.

The stories came courtesy of Lester Lewis, who had roomed with Bucky at Vanderbilt. Eleanor had hired Lester as her number two. He was a meticulous draftsman who'd grown up on a thoroughbred farm in Kentucky but was afraid of ponies. It was his idea to give the ponies of *Looper Wash* their ornery personalities.

"Grr," Eleanor said, erasing the eyes on a laughing Millicent. "I'm terrible at eyes."

It was 2003. *Looper Wash* was still a month from airing but the animators had been working for two years in a loft on the dodgy end of Broome Street. Eleanor had her own office, but she preferred the bullpen, working side by side with her New York team. Scores more artists hand-painted in Hungary.

"Is there anything likeable about your friend Bucky?" Eleanor asked.

Lester had to think about it. "He's loyal."

"But you can't genuinely like him," Eleanor said, raising Millicent's lower lids in an attempt to give her that smiling-eye look.

"We're devoted friends," Lester cried. "We speak every day."

"Does he know you mock him behind his back?"

"I mock him to his face!" Lester said gleefully.

Eleanor's team was color-correcting, making last-minute changes and throwing in topical jokes to season one, getting animatic notes on season two, and storyboarding season three. It was high-stress and sedentary work; fourteen-hour days hunched over drawing boards, vacations canceled, out-of-town parents stood up at fancy restaurants, weddings postponed, births of babies just missed.

In the stranglehold of deadlines, a bunker mentality set in. The animators versus the idiot network executives; versus the capricious and overpaid writers; versus the incompetent and venal Hungarians.

The one bright spot in the animators' day occurred after lunch when Lester would return from his daily phone call with Bucky and recount the highlights in delicious detail. For the next hour, a calm settled over the bullpen as the animators dissected Bucky across their light boards.

Did they love him? Hate him? They took extravagant pleasure in the debate.

If only there were some way to hear his voice!

Eleanor suggested they get the phone guy to add Lester's line to the speakerphone in her office so the animators could pile in and listen in on him and Bucky.

"Please?" Eleanor asked Lester. "He's all we have."

A rush order was submitted.

Bucky didn't disappoint.

"I'm every shade of aggravated." Bucky at home, settling onto his daybed after an especially rich lunch. His voice was confident and strangely accent-free.

Eleanor passed a note to Lester. *Why doesn't he have a Southern accent?*

Lester nodded and gave Eleanor a wink.

"Bucky," Lester said. "The other night I started to explain to someone your philosophy on Southern accents, but all I could remember was that it defied logic."

"Southern accents are hillbilly," Bucky said with petulance. "Anyone with a proper education, I don't care if he's never stepped foot out of the South, doesn't go around sounding like Jubilation T. Cornpone. If he does, it's a put-on. And please, I'm in no mood to rehash the obvious. I've just had a knock-down, drag-out with the mail lady."

"No kidding," Lester said.

"As you know, I had a mailbox made for the carriage house. Last week I left a note stating that from now on, all mail addressed to Barnaby Fanning was to be delivered there. Every day it's been empty. Today I confronted her, and she said that by law anything addressed to 2658 Coliseum had to be put in Mummy and Daddy's box. If I wanted mail in a different box, I'd need a different address. She kindly suggested I traipse down to city hall and have the carriage house designated 2658 A. Can you imagine? Barnaby Fortune Charbonneau Fanning, 2658 A! She obviously doesn't know."

(This Buckyism worked its way into *Looper Wash*. Season two, episode twenty. Josh, the kindly and patient sheriff, refused to arrest a drifter for stealing the girls' rock tumbler. Vivian stormed off, saying of Josh, "She obviously doesn't know.")

"Perhaps," Lester said, "the post lady would have been more accommodating if you'd given her actual money for Christmas instead of re-gifted potpourri."

"I suppose next year I could throw in some car-wash coupons," Bucky said dryly, playing along.

"He's addictive, this guy!" Eleanor said after they'd hung up.

February drew near. The anticipation became palpable. Not for the premiere of *Looper Wash* but for Mardi Gras and Bucky's account of riding on the Khaos float. Could he possibly deliver after all the hype?

"Standing there in my white tights and sparkling shoes, my gold lamé shorts, silk mask, and hair wig—"

What's a hair wig? someone scribbled on the whiteboard. Nobody knew.

"—tossing beads to the lowly throngs, ten-deep between me and the blue wall of Porta-Potties, entire families with their Deuce McAllister jerseys, acid-dyed shorts, and eighteen-dollar haircuts, springing up from their lawn chairs, knocking over their hibachis, heads back, mouths open like baby sparrows, fingers grabbing at the air, hoping for a lucky throw." He paused to marinate in the memory. "I know how Lindbergh must have felt."

Eleanor's boyfriend, Joe, had dropped by to take her to lunch. He entered during the tail end of Bucky's monologue and was violently shushed.

When the call ended, the room exploded in victorious whoops.

"Bucky," Eleanor explained to Joe. "You gotta love him."

"Do I?"

A week later, the animators were huddled in Eleanor's office.

"Your big three-oh is coming up, Mr. Lewis," Bucky said from the speaker. "What are our plans?"

"Eleanor is throwing me a party at her place."

"Your boss Eleanor?" A sniff could be heard from the speaker.

"Do you have a cold coming on?" Lester asked with a wink to the busting-a-gut animators.

"Remind me of her last name," Bucky said.

"Flood. She's related to President John Tyler."

"A direct descendant?"

"Her mother's name was Tess Tyler," Lester said, looking over at Eleanor to make sure that was correct. "Eleanor has a pair of John Tyler's derringers in her apartment to prove it."

"A direct descendant of a U.S. president in show business? I must witness such a travesty firsthand. Inform her I'll be attending her little fête."

It was the captain of Khaos himself, riding his comet to New York City. Eleanor's team did what all feral and procrastinating animators did: they came up with a wager.

Everyone put in a twenty and whoever came the closest to drawing an accurate Bucky would win the pot. (The Internet has since fiercely debated why the Looper Four were so sloppily rendered in the "Guitar Zan" episode. The answer: Bucky Fanning.)

Most of the Buckys submitted were stump-sized. Some bow-tied gentlemen-of-yore. One a drooly, fly-swarmed hayseed. Eleanor settled on average height, balding, driving moccasins, no socks, wool pants, floral button-down and lavender cashmere sweater tied loosely around the shoulders. She threw in oversized Versace aviators with gradient lenses.

The day arrived. Bucky strode into Eleanor's office. Bucky in the flesh.

He was indisputably handsome: tall, perfect skin, sensual lips, luxuriant wavy hair. (Lester had often insisted Bucky was attractive. "So why can't he get a date?" Eleanor had asked. "He doesn't want *a date*," Lester explained. "He wants someone who won't leave him.")

Bucky wore black. Black bomber jacket, black cashmere crewneck with a black silk T-shirt peeking above, black leather ankle boots with the red Prada stripe up the heel. Slightly ridiculous, but only if you knew Bucky was a social cripple with no job. Otherwise, he looked like any other wealthy hipster on the streets of SoHo.

More than anything, Bucky had an imposing presence. He wasn't fat, exactly. He reminded Eleanor of how papayas swelled during the rainy season or the way Greg Gumbel looked like someone had taken a bicycle pump to Bryant Gumbel.

Bucky's eyes immediately landed on the twenties spilling out of a wire in-basket.

"What's the bet?" he asked.

Panicky eyes swung to Eleanor.

"There's no bet," she answered too quickly.

"There's a bet," Bucky said calmly.

Beside Eleanor on the couch sat a coffee filter filled with honey-mustard pretzel nuggets. Her hand reached for one. Bucky took in Eleanor for a beat and nodded, as if that told him all he needed to know. He turned to Lester.

"I made us a lunch reservation at Balthazar, Mr. Lewis. I presume that is up to your middling standards."

It should have come as no surprise to Eleanor that at Lester's party, her baby sister, Ivy, Ivy the willowy, translucent one with a fluttery aura (she was the air and Eleanor was the earth), Ivy six foot one in ninth grade, who, a month before high-school graduation went to model in Paris and then Japan but had no luck in New York, where it mattered, who followed an acting coach to the Berkshires which ended up being a cult and had to be rescued by Eleanor and her then-boyfriend Joe, Ivy who miraculously booked a Dior campaign so her face was all over the subways one summer but lost all that money and her modeling connections in an ironically named Ponzi scheme, "Friends Helping Friends," Ivy who hitchhiked to Telluride for an ayahuasca ceremony and stayed three years shacking up with the shaman, Mestre Mike, next finding religion in *Fat Is a Feminist Issue, Toxic Parents,* and *Healing the Shame That Binds You,* this Ivy, who became a certified masseuse but quit because the constant transfer of bad energy was making her weak, she was allergic to wheat and cut out sugar before anyone was allergic to wheat and cut out sugar, she also refused to eat meat because it was biting into animal screams and she avoided nuts because viruses clung to nuts, the Ivy whose skin had become flaky and eye sockets saggy, who couldn't shake her angry dry cough, who Eleanor's by-then-husband Joe, a surgeon who knew a dying bulimic when he saw one, checked into an eating-disorder unit on Second Avenue where Ivy was forced on arrival to eat a sloppy joe on a white bun, despite sobbing and gagging and collapsing on the linoleum floor, Ivy who was now answering phones for David Parry, rock-and-roll manager and husband of Violet, the head writer of *Looper Wash*, as a personal favor to Eleanor, Ivy who was now thirty-three and healthy if getting a little old for her act, it was this Ivy who came to Lester's party, it was this Ivy who met Bucky, captivated Bucky, went back to the St. Regis with Bucky, and to New Orleans the next day.

A year later they were married.

The engagement party was held in New Orleans.

One of Joe's rules: The first thing you do in a new city is take the public transportation. He and Eleanor chugged along St. Charles in the overstuffed streetcar. From afar, the live oaks seemed to drip with Spanish moss, but up close, they were just Mardi Gras beads, months old, stuck there.

Eleanor and Joe hopped off at Third Street and crossed. The Fanning estate was on the good side of the avenue, the river side.

2658 Coliseum stretched the entire block, its iron fence skillfully wrought into stalks of sugarcane. A plaque told the history, but it was too dark out to read.

The mansion glowed from within. Eleanor balked at the gate.

The disbelief had been hitting her in waves since she'd gotten the news that Bucky had proposed to Ivy on the plane to New Orleans. ("All I require is that you love oysters," he'd told her. "But I don't love oysters." "You will.") Eleanor had shown up at work that Monday, her in-basket still rich with twenties. Nobody had the heart to claim them. The joke wasn't funny anymore.

Lester had marched manfully into Eleanor's office. "There's a good chance it won't work out—"

"I'm happy for them," Eleanor said and returned to her work. "Could you close the door?"

The mansion door swung open courtesy of a courtly black man in tails with white hair and white gloves. He was Mister, the husband of Taffy. Both uniformed servants to two generations of Fannings, and hopefully a third, now that Bucky had returned from New York with, of all things, a bride.

Eleanor and Joe entered. The living room was a-swish with ball gowns and tails. Just as an "Oh!" was about to escape Eleanor's mouth—she'd worn flats and a knee-length dress she'd had no time to iron—a mint julep was thrust into her palm. The shock of the frosty silver tumbler slapped Eleanor's face into a smile.

"Eleanor! Joe!" It was Ivy, wearing a pleated chiffon gown, lime with orange flowers and sleeves that hung like calla lilies. She gave it a twirl. "1972 Lilly Pulitzer! It belonged to Bucky's mother. Did you know that if you admire something, the person has to give it to you? That's the Southern way."

Ivy took Eleanor's hand and introduced her around. Ivy's frailty was still there, but without the undercurrent of unpredictability. No, being adored by Bucky—and she was adored, no question, the way his soft gaze infused her with ease, the delight they took in each other's words, the way his forearm fit the curve of her waist—had softened Ivy's edges. One might say she'd grown into her frailty. The South was a good place for that.

Politicians and oil barons, lawyers and historians, shipping titans and ne'er-do-wells: to a person, they loved Ivy, had fully embraced her and, by association, Eleanor and Joe. Eleanor had never before felt so fascinating. In turn, those she spoke with became fascinating, and so the bonhomie spiraled up, up, up. The air felt cozy with kindness and laughter, not like New York, where people you talked to perpetually scanned the room for someone better. A week earlier, at a Fox network party, a *Simpsons* writer had literally pushed Eleanor aside midsentence when James L. Brooks walked in behind her. Manners, Eleanor grasped through the haze of mint juleps, weren't a function of hollow snobbery and misguided airs; they were acts of profound generosity.

Granny Charbonneau sat sternly in the corner, both hands firmly gripping the long handle of her cane. At one point she flapped her hand at Eleanor.

"Are you the sister?" Granny Charbonneau barked. "Maybe you can convince Bucky to stop dressing like a hangman."

At the food table, Eleanor couldn't get enough of the hot spinach dip. Taffy leaned in and shared the secret ingredient: "Campbell's Cream of Mushroom."

Bucky's mother led Joe over. "This one I just want to slip in my pocket." Earlier in the day, she'd cut her forearm sharpening the blade of the push mower. "Mister hurt his back, and what's the alternative, to hire a team of gardeners? I can cut my own lawn."

Later, Eleanor found herself alone. She dropped into a fussy love seat. The pillows hit her low back in just the right spot. Mary Marge leaped onto her lap and curled up.

"Hello, you," Eleanor said to the pooch, startled by how thick-tongued it came out. She was unaccustomed to the relentless salvos of alcohol.

Chunky leather scrapbooks lined the coffee table, their sumptuous padded covers begging to be opened. Eleanor obliged. On the first page was a truly weird photo.

The Royal Court of Khaos.

Grown men and women in outlandish costumes, their faces morbidly serious, more waxen than human. Bucky, in a beaded gold satin shirt, gold shorts, white tights, rouged cheeks, a platinum-blond Prince Valiant (hair?) wig and a fountain of ostrich feathers springing from his gold headpiece, stood among the similarly lurid king, queen, pages, and maidens.

"Those parties start in a month." It was Ivy, with Bucky. "I couldn't be more nervous. Bucky's making me take curtsying lessons so I don't embarrass him before the court."

"Ivy, my love," Bucky said with mock exhaustion. "They're not parties. They're balls."

"Finally! Someone to do all my thinking for me!" Ivy mimed plucking her head off her shoulders and handing it to Bucky.

"Bucky," Eleanor said, straining to enunciate, "I want to thank you for making my sister so happy."

"My life will have been a failure if spent making your sister *happy*," Bucky boomed. "I won't rest until the sun and the moon redden with shame knowing Ivy outshines them both."

"We're flying to Italy to have me fitted for white gloves," Ivy said. "If you're sitting in the front row, the gloves have to be over the elbow. Don't you love it?"

"It's *on* the front row, darling," Bucky said. "One sits *on* the front row."

Joe had a nickname for Ivy: "the Monstrance." On certain Catholic holy days, the Eucharist was displayed in a golden-sunburst monstrance where worshipful eyes gazed at it around the clock. Joe, an altar boy, had often been tasked with the graveyard shift. In Bucky, this living monstrance, Ivy, had found her perpetual adoration.

Eleanor's shoulders melted. Something deep in her jaw loosened. Ivy was going to be okay.

Their mother had died at St. Vincent's. Those final visits, once so vivid in Eleanor's mind, had faded with time. The old woman in the next bed being wheeled out for hip surgery, then wheeled back in thirty minutes later when they didn't have the right instruments. The bag of dark urine hanging from the bed rail. Their mother, the Broadway star, dry-mouthed and distant. On one of her last visits, Eleanor had brought a picture she'd drawn: Tess with a grown-up Ivy and Eleanor, all three improbably wearing wedding dresses. "This is lovely, Eleanor," her mother whispered. "But it won't work."

Eleanor cherished the memories of her mother: being picked up at school by Tess in her dance clothes and blue fedora, fringe purse swinging at her hip; listening to Tess, Gigi, and Alan gossip outrageously about the other dancers in the company, Eleanor not quite following but oh, the thrill of joining in the laughter; the parties that ended with everyone standing around the piano singing show tunes; the Cornish game hens for dinner; the exotic scent of Erno Laszlo facial products; the dazzling contents of her jewelry drawer; the lazy afternoons at the Bowlmor.

But these recollected moments also carried extreme guilt. Eleanor was old enough to remember how much Tess enjoyed her company, how unhurried their moments were together. Ivy remembered only the abandonment.

"Please don't hold it against me," Bucky told Eleanor, "but the future Mrs. Fanning and I must beg our exit. The *Times-Picayune* has arrived."

With Bucky gone, ruddy-cheeked Joe joined Eleanor.

"Wow," he said, the pillow hitting his back in the sweet spot.

"I know."

"Make room, make room." Lorraine, Bucky's second cousin, nestled between them. "Get that rat off you." She pushed a snoozing Mary Marge onto the floor and waved over some champagne.

"Can you believe how seriously everyone takes this?" Lorraine said of the scrapbooks. She opened up to her year. There she was, the Queen of Khaos. "Look how thin I was! I know what y'all are thinking, it's moneyed tomfoolery, and you're not wrong, but I tell you, it's a gas!"

Across the room, Bucky arranged Ivy's train for a photographer. Behind them hung a portrait of Bucky's ancestor P.G.T. Beauregard, the Confederate general who ordered the first shot fired in the War Between the States.

"Oh, Barnaby!" Lorraine said with a mixture of fondness and spite. "Anytime he vexes you, and he will vex you, just remember, he's a Troubled Troubadour. It's a nickname we gave him. We were in the car when Kurt Cobain shot himself. The announcer came on the radio and said, 'Troubled troubadour Kurt Cobain has been found dead'... The name just stuck, Troubled Troubadour. He's not so bad once you realize it gives him great comfort to know where he stands."

It was Irish coffee now, and who wasn't comforted by knowing where they stood? The birds with the cascading tail feathers on the wallpaper, the butter-colored ceiling, the gold mirrors and jute rugs: the effect wasn't pretentious, it was comforting, just like the blue-and-white striped love seat. Who would have thought blue-and-white stripes went with butter and birds and gold and jute, but it worked. So did being looked in the eye when people spoke to you, and teens in tuxes conversing with adults. Why *not* waiters in tails and white gloves? Why not Bucky's mother and her friends in decades-old dresses, sun-damaged skin, frosted lipstick, and low chunky heels? Why not flowers from the garden and dinged julep tumblers and food that was good but not great? When Dixieland music started playing, the splash of the trumpet and belch of the tuba confused Eleanor at first because it was clearly live but not coming from inside. Then, faintly through the garden windows, Eleanor made them out: joyous black kids in short sleeves and neckties playing for the party, outside so it wouldn't be too noisy. They could see in but Eleanor couldn't see out. Why not that too?

The next morning, the jagged double ring of the hotel phone startled Eleanor awake. It was Ivy, tentative, asking how Eleanor had slept but not wanting to know how Eleanor had slept. Bucky was upset about the cachepot.

"What's a cachepot?"

"You don't know what a cachepot is?" Ivy said. "It's a porcelain pot for hiding things. Last night the ice cream was meant to go in one. Instead, it got plunked down on the sideboard in its carton. In the *Times-Picayune* this morning you can see it, bold as life, right there among the Charbonneau china. Dreyer's."

Eleanor vaguely recalled. When the bananas Foster was served, someone had asked for ice cream. At the time, Taffy had been on hands and knees working on a wine spill, so Eleanor went into the kitchen and set the ice cream out herself…

"I know," Ivy said. "We finally got to the bottom of it."

Was this a joke?

"You made Bucky look like a philistine on a night that should have been a celebration of our engagement."

"It *was* a celebration of your engagement." Eleanor sat up in bed. Nausea welled.

There was an odd hesitation before Ivy spoke. Was it Bucky? Whispering?

"It was an insult to Bucky," Ivy said. "It was an insult to his parents, and, worse, it was an insult to Taffy."

"Taffy?" Eleanor said. "I was trying to help Taffy."

"That's just it," Ivy said. "Taffy doesn't need your help."

"I'm sure she didn't take it as an insult."

"Bucky did and I did."

Joe was awake now and shaking his head.

"Put Bucky on the phone," Eleanor said, tears coming down in sheets. "I'll apologize."

"He doesn't want to get on the phone."

"I'll apologize in person, at breakfast."

Another weird pause. "It's been a long night around here, waiting for the *Times-Picayune* to be delivered. Anyway, it's the type of thing that should be done in writing. You can leave a letter with the concierge."

Eleanor flew to the desk and clawed at the sliver of a drawer, wild for stationery. Joe had his running shoes on.

"It didn't work for Neville Chamberlain," he said. And then he headed out.

John Tyler, a Virginia legislator, was added to William Henry Harrison's Whig ticket solely to deliver the Southern vote. When Harrison was sworn in on a freezing 1841 day, Tyler attended the inauguration. That evening, he returned to his plantation in Virginia, expecting few vice-presidential duties. A month later, a hand-delivered letter informed him that Harrison had died of pneumonia, making John Tyler the tenth president of the United States. Tyler, nicknamed "His Accidency," governed without distinction. He chose not to run for reelection and, when his term was over, returned to the family plantation, Sherwood Forest. Because he accomplished so little in office, John Tyler is known in history books mainly for being the president who fathered the most children, fifteen. Because he was later elected to the Confederate congress, Tyler is also known for being the only president upon whose death the nation's flag did not fly at half-mast.

Sherwood Forest is open to the public, although few tourists find reason to take the trip down Route 5, the John Tyler Highway, to the tidewater of Charles City County, Virginia. Astonishingly, John Tyler's grandson is still alive and resides there with his wife. Sherwood Forest's house, at three hundred feet, is the longest frame house in the country. It includes a seventy-foot-by-twelve-foot ballroom designed for the Virginia reel, Tyler's favorite dance. Sherwood Forest's sixteen hundred acres are dotted with former smokehouses, stables, and slave quarters. The twenty-five acres of terraced gardens include hundred-foot magnolias and maples as well as the first *Gingko biloba* tree planted in the United States, a gift to Tyler from Commodore Perry. Over the years, the Tyler family have received countless requests to rent Sherwood Forest for private parties. They've always declined.

Which was why, when Bucky Fanning phoned the Tylers with a request to get married at Sherwood Forest and was refused, once, twice, and three times, after which he got on a plane to Atlanta and drove the seven hours to Charles City County to make a personal appeal and the Tylers said yes, every toast at the rehearsal dinner mentioned this as quintessential Bucky.

"Either run with the big dogs or stay on the porch," someone said.

Bucky. You really did have to love him.

Khaos's party planner oversaw the June wedding. She spent the day itself welcoming a fleet of vans to Sherwood Forest carrying straight–from–New Orleans oysters, crawfish, milk rolls, and the full Jimmy Maxwell Orchestra. She was also tasked with navigating the delicate challenge of having a hundred and sixty-four guests on the groom's side and two on the bride's.

The afternoon of the nuptials, Ivy and Eleanor lolled in Richmond Inn robes, Joe having just returned from a day trip to Monticello. In two hours, the bridal shuttle would ferry them to Sherwood Forest.

Ivy, always the chameleon, spoke with a Southern lilt.

"I was lying in bed one morning. You know my favorite thing in creation is an after-breakfast nap..."

Ivy took center stage on the vast expanse of beige carpet. Her eyes danced with wicked amusement. Had she learned it from Eleanor, the ability to turn any event into a story?

"I swear to you, the wallpaper started moving. I got out of bed and put my hand on the spot and it was warm! I found a pucker in the seam and pulled. Underneath were mud tubes, like veins crawling up the wall. I screamed like the star of a teen horror movie. 'Termites!'"

Ivy's endless leg peeked through the high slit in her bathrobe, an effect so sexy it might have been staged; for Ivy, these alluring moments happened of themselves.

"Not a week later I went to mail a letter and the mailbox fell off its post. Right into the street! A group of tourists were standing around reading that old plaque and I just about died of embarrassment."

Joe grabbed a video camera to capture this, Ivy at her best. There had been bad times but there were good ones too.

"The next day, the termites swarmed the carriage house, thousands of them in a cloud you couldn't see through. That's how they mate, in flight! Poor Taffy had to stand there with a vacuum sucking them out of the air. They got in her eyes and her ears and her nostrils! She was spitting them out of her mouth! You know what else? After termites mate, their wings drop off. So for the rest of the year, wings in my cereal, wings in my slippers. Once I squirted sunblock in my hand and there were wings in it! The craziest part? You mention termites to anyone in New Orleans and they're in utter denial. 'What termites?' We had to call the Terminix guy because they'd gotten into the two-by-four things that hold up the roof. Bucky made him park around the corner. But when the neighbor came home and saw the Terminix truck in front of *his* house, he marched over, and he and Bucky had it out on the front lawn. Even after that, you mention termites and Bucky will say, 'What termites?'"

Ivy sat on Joe's lap and threw her arms around his neck. "Oh, Joe." They fell back on the bed. "You've always been there for me. I've been such a disaster. The good news is after tonight, I'll be Bucky's problem."

Bucky had entered. It was unclear how much he'd heard.

He stiffly addressed Eleanor. "As you know, in keeping with Tyler tradition, my first dance with your sister will be the Virginia reel." He set a piece of paper on a bureau near the door. "Here are your places for it."

The door clicked shut. A choking silence filled the suite. Eleanor spoke first.

"Okay, Joe, your turn to bust out the hotel stationery."

"That's not funny." Ivy sat up and swung her legs around the side of the bed, darkness rising.

Joe pointed to the suitcase. Eleanor nodded, went to it, took out a present.

"From me to you!" Eleanor said, and sat next to Ivy. She turned to Joe. "Honey, cover your ears." She took Ivy's hand. "Men will come and go. But we'll always be sisters."

From the weight of the box, Ivy's face exploded into a smile.

"I know what this is!" Ivy sang. "John Tyler's derringers! Bucky bet me a nickel!"

"Actually, no. It's not the derringers."

Eleanor had thought it right for the new couple to have at least one scrapbook devoted to Ivy's family. As their father kept no photos from their childhood, Eleanor had hand-drawn some of her own, as well as a map of Aspen.

It had taken all her spare time for months. Eleanor was still feeling the physical toll: the frozen right shoulder, the aching eyes, the stomach lining eaten by coffee and ibuprofen.

As a final touch, Eleanor had ordered the leather scrapbook from a stationery shop in the French Quarter. For its spine she had a small silver plaque engraved, in Fanning-family font: THE FLOOD GIRLS.

"This is good too," Ivy said.

"I have just the person you should meet!" said Quentin.

Eleanor was back in New Orleans, in Bucky and Ivy's carriage house. They'd been married a year. Quentin was a rumpled gentleman with a full-on Southern drawl who took impish delight in every word Eleanor spoke. She'd just told him she was Ivy's sister, an animator from New York.

Quentin scurried off to find a pen and paper, leaving Eleanor standing in the living room facing the window treatments. Valance, curtains, swag, Roman shade, and blackout roller. Five separate things. Six, if you counted the silk tassels.

Bucky came by sipping a screwdriver and joined Eleanor at the window.

"Maroon and ivory is my favorite color story," he explained.

"Color story?" Eleanor said, snapping out of her trance.

"One is a color," Bucky said. "Two or more is a color story. Surely you know that." And he left.

A dozen family and friends were gathered around the derringers, newly mounted on the wall above a plaque boasting their provenance. After Bucky and Ivy had named their baby John-Tyler, Eleanor felt she had no option but to give them the pair of guns. Joe, sitting in a low chair in the corner of the antique-choked living room, had a different opinion.

Quentin returned with a cocktail napkin.

"If you're in animation, there's a fellow you should meet,"

Quentin said. "Bucky's dear friend from Vandy. He draws that show we all love with the girls on the ponies."

He handed Eleanor a cocktail napkin with a name in Sharpie. *Lester Lewis.*

"Lester Lewis?" Eleanor said. "Lester works for me. Hang on a second. Bucky told you his friend Lester works on *Looper Wash* but failed to mention I'm his boss?"

"Ooh, it looks like I stepped in something," Quentin said, and tiptoed off.

There were no books in the house, only a shelf of scrapbooks. Eleanor scanned the spines. LE DÉBUT DES JEUNES FILLES 1998; COURT OF KHAOS 1998; SHERWOOD FOREST 2004; BIRTH OF JOHN-TYLER 2005 —

"The priest is waiting!" It was Ivy. "We have a very short window." Tiny, pink John-Tyler slept in her arms, his antique lace christening gown so long, a uniformed nurse had to carry the train.

St. Louis Cathedral, "the cathedral" to locals, is the oldest in North America. It's a favorite spot for tourists to cool off; the church remains open to the public even during weddings, christenings, and funerals.

Inside, thirty family members stood in the front with hymnals; Joe, the atheist holdout, waited outside.

During the ceremony, it was a challenge to hear Father Bowman's blessings of John-Tyler Barnaby Fortune Gammill Charbonneau Fanning over the competing bands in Jackson Square. Every time the church door opened, the family got a blast of the ubiquitous "When the Saints Go Marching In." The proceedings had to be paused after a chicken was spotted in the nave and tourists surged in to take photos. One knocked over Granny Charbonneau's cane. During the lull, Eleanor found herself next to Bucky needing something to say.

"You're really going all in with this John Tyler connection."

It was the tone of Eleanor's voice that caught the ears of the family. Bucky stared at her, perfectly composed, his eyes daring her to continue.

"It's too bad he was the worst president," Eleanor said. "Did you know his death was the only time the Capitol didn't fly the flag at half-mast for a president?"

Now even tourists were straining to hear. Eleanor thought she'd throw in something extra, a *lagniappe*, they call it in New Orleans.

"With fifteen children," Eleanor said, "the question isn't who *is* a direct descendant of John Tyler. The question is, who *isn't*. I mean, half the people here." She lazily gestured to the tourists in their tank tops.

Bucky's face reddened. No further eye contact was made.

Out on the steps, Eleanor found Joe leaning on a column in the stifling heat.

"You made the right decision," she said with a kiss.

Ivy flitted out and squeezed their arms.

"Listen, y'all. J.T. hasn't been sleeping through the night. I think we're going to go home, just the three of us."

Bleary-eyed tourists shuffled down Bourbon Street carrying daiquiris in giant bong-like things. The stench of last night's vomit lingered despite that morning's convoy of water-spraying trucks followed by a foot brigade of men with push brooms, scrubbing. Three kids in shorts and porkpie hats meandered; at their sides dangled a slide trombone, trumpet, and white bucket that rattled with a pair of drumsticks. Waiters in tuxedos and cooks in whites leaned against the fronts of restaurants, smoking or just taking in the lazy river of humanity. There were no alleys in the French Quarter, so waiters, cooks, and shopkeepers took their breaks on the sidewalks. On one side of the street a kid had attached tops of soda cans to the soles of his unlaced Air Jordans. He tapped in a loose-limbed burst and then stood there. His friend across the street answered back. Neither seemed particularly committed. A man rode slowly by on a too-small bicycle, knees out like chicken wings, one hand on the handlebars, the other gripping a tangle of fishing rods. Three plastic milk crates were parked in the street, unclaimed. The kids with the instruments shrugged and sat down on them. The heat was getting to everyone.

Joe and Eleanor walked along trying to find Preservation Hall, the venerable home of New Orleans jazz. Joe didn't care for New Orleans jazz—he found it hokey and good-timey—but was determined to salvage the trip by seeing something of historic value. Eleanor followed, her feet sinking into the hot asphalt with every step.

"You think Bucky would have married her if she weren't descended from a president? Remember at the wedding when everyone was congratulating me on the Emmy nominations? I was watching Bucky. He couldn't stand it! He's never once acknowledged what I do. But of course he'll boast about his friend Lester from Vanderbilt. And what is Vanderbilt? I've barely even heard of it."

"Before you met the guy, all you heard was that he was an

asshole," Joe said. "His cousin warned us he was an asshole. At his wedding, every toast alluded to him being an asshole. And now you're surprised he's an asshole?"

"I wish I'd never given them those derringers," she said.

"I can't talk about the derringers."

They arrived on the corner of Bourbon and St. Peter under a sign, MAISON BOURBON FOR THE PRESERVATION OF JAZZ. Eleanor started inside.

"This isn't it," Joe said.

"It says 'Preservation'—" Eleanor said.

"It's not Preservation Hall."

"But there's a band—"

"Preservation Hall wouldn't have neon frozen daiquiris with names like Irish Car Bomb. And its band wouldn't be playing 'Sara Smile.'"

"You don't have to yell at me."

Joe's jaw was going.

"I'm going to find Preservation Hall," he said. "Come with me or don't. But of all the things that odious buffoon has gotten away with, I won't let him add to the list causing me to fight with my wife in the middle of Bourbon Street!" He stalked off.

Eleanor might have gone after Joe, but she spotted Lorraine and her two boys crossing Bourbon Street a block away. Eleanor couldn't tell if Lorraine had made eye contact under her hat.

A moment later, Eleanor saw an older woman in a long Pucci dress headed down the same side street. She remembered the dress from the church.

Strange. Eleanor walked to the corner. Both women were gone. Perhaps they'd slipped into a place called Antoine's.

Under the restaurant sign, a door led to a cavernous dining room with mirrored walls, tile floors, and tables for ten with white tablecloths. It was empty but for waiters in black bow ties and waistcoats sitting in one corner folding napkins. In the opposite corner, a door with yellow glass. Behind it, the movement of people. Eleanor's steps echoed as she clacked toward the door. The waiters looked up and continued folding.

Deeper in was an even larger dining room with a carved wooden ceiling, this one pulsing with patrons, the clang of dishes, and good cheer. Celebrity photos in dusty frames covered every inch of the red pillars and walls. Waiters with aprons down to their shins carried trays with one hand and blotted their brows with the other.

Eleanor's eyes raced from table to table. No Lorraine, no woman in Pucci.

Behind her, a white glass globe, lit from within. On it, the silhouette of a woman with high-piled hair. FEMMES.

Inside the ladies' lounge, Eleanor slumped into a tired velvet chair and closed her eyes. She wasn't thinking straight. The fight with Joe. The scrum with Bucky. The goddamned heat.

She opened her eyes.

A woman in a wrap dress washed her hands. The counter was so worn that a puddle had collected across its expanse. The woman dried her hands and dropped the paper towel on an overflowing trash can. In the mirror, her plastic tiara. On it, in fake jewels, the reverse letters *J.T.*

There was no way.

The door shut.

Eleanor went after her. The tiara'd woman was halfway across the noisy dining room. Before Eleanor could catch up, she vanished into a wall of newspaper clippings. A jib door. Eleanor pushed it open.

She found herself in a dim hallway even denser with photos and made narrow by display cases on either side. The floors were shellacked brick, the walls dark wood. Doors made of thick red glass and elaborate wrought iron. To her left, a photo of Pope John Paul II standing in the kitchen with Antoine himself. On display, the plate the Pope had eaten from.

The woman had disappeared again, this time into the shadow at the end of the hall. Eleanor felt herself pulled toward voices. Above the doors on her left and right, plaques reading REX and PROTEUS. One room was green, the other purple. Eleanor could make out gilded displays of queens' costumes: ermine capes, crowns, and scepters. Even in the dark, their jewels threw off glints of light.

Around the corner, at the end of the hall, a cracked door. Above it, in ghostly white letters, KHAOS.

News of Eleanor's presence had preceded her. Ivy appeared in the doorway, blocking Eleanor's view of the sheer number of people in attendance, many more than at the christening.

"You said—" Eleanor stammered. "I thought the three of you were going home."

Through the crowd, Bucky, with Mary Marge tucked in his elbow, offered the hint of a smile and returned to his conversation.

"I didn't know how to tell you," Ivy said. "We decided this should be family only."

*

Eleanor fled across the street into an aggressively air-conditioned praline shop, minimalist and empty of customers. Her perspiration instantly froze, causing a violent shudder.

"Would you like a sample?" asked an angular woman with flat black hair.

"Sure," Eleanor said, straining to seem like a normal patron. The woman handed her a frosted pecan. The tears began. Eleanor turned her back and stood too close to a red shelf filled with jars of praline sauce.

The door jingled. Ivy grabbed Eleanor's arm and spun her around.

"You have no idea how hard it is for me to be caught between you and Bucky," Ivy said, her face pleading.

"Between me and Bucky?" Eleanor said. "What did I do to him? Fly down here and miss my final animatic of the season? Drag my husband to a christening even though we're both atheists?"

"It's not what you've done to him," Ivy said. "It's what you've done to me. You didn't come down for my birthday."

Before Eleanor could process this, Ivy backpedaled. "I know, I know—I never expected you to. But it's how Bucky thinks." She gave a worried sigh, then in a rush, "He's never gotten over you ruining our engagement party."

"We're still on Cachepotgate?" Eleanor said. The praline she'd been clutching had turned to goo in her hot palm.

"It started before," Ivy said. "When you walked into the party. You saw how people were dressed and you asked where everyone was going."

"I did not," Eleanor said, remembering the moment clearly. "I certainly *thought* it because it looked like opening night at the opera. But I know for a fact I didn't *say* anything."

"Bucky heard you."

With that, a line had been drawn. Eleanor drew lines for a living. She knew one when she saw one.

She walked to the register and forced a smile. "May I have a napkin, please?"

The woman reached under the counter and tore off a paper towel. Eleanor scrubbed the sticky sugar off her fingers. She placed the pecan in the towel and handed it back. "Thank you."

"Oh no!" Ivy came around to see Eleanor's face. "Are you mad?"

"This might get loud, and that wouldn't be fair to the praline shop." With that, Eleanor pushed past her sister and out the door.

"Okay, let's do this," Eleanor said to Ivy out on the sidewalk. "Where's the scrapbook I made you? Where's my goddamn wedding present?"

"As you know, we expected the derringers."

"You do realize this isn't you talking?" Eleanor said.

"They were Mom's," Ivy said. "They belong to me as much as they belong to you. They're the only things left of hers. You just had them lying around your apartment."

"What was I supposed to do? Ship them to you care of Mestre Mike's yurt?"

"Bucky and I got married at John Tyler's house so it should have been obvious," Ivy said, unshaken.

"You got the derringers!" Eleanor said. "Last time I checked, they were mounted on your wall."

"We should have gotten them before." Ivy raised her face in defiance. It was a peculiar gesture for her, one Eleanor had never seen.

"You didn't answer my question," Eleanor said. "Where's *The Flood Girls*?"

"Bucky and I were both offended by *The Flood Girls*."

"Ivy, I'm warning you: don't."

"We don't know what's so charming about a bear crashing around a house while children are sleeping—"

"It's our life, Ivy. It's us."

"—or waiting in a car while Ted Bundy is on the loose. And why on earth would you make me relive Parsley being hit by a car? You know how much I loved that dog."

"I loved Parsley too!" Eleanor said. "Okay, I get it. Bucky feeds on insults and now he's got you doing the same."

"I finally found a man who treats me the way I deserve," Ivy said. "You're allowed to have that, but I'm not? And where was Joe during the christening?"

"Now Bucky has a problem with Joe?"

"Eleanor, *everybody* noticed Joe wouldn't come inside."

"Joe was tormented by nuns as a child and he's not a fan of the Catholic Church. You know that!"

"You," Ivy said. "Mocking the namesake of our son in front of tourists. Oh, Eleanor, even I couldn't defend your sarcasm. I can see it in your eyes, when you're going in for the kill. You delight in your nastiness and you always take it out on those weaker than you. I'm done with it and so is Bucky."

"I have a message for that walking joke—"

"Eleanor," Ivy said. "You're talking about my husband. Bucky is my husband."

"Tell him he's won," Eleanor said, reddening. "The two of you will have to find someone else to mine for grievances. Because this is the last time you see me. Watch how serious I am."

Preservation Hall was thirty feet by thirty feet. The walls were water-stained and covered with pegboard; the thick wood planks had survived their share of floods. There was no stage. Only fifty listeners could pack in; those on mangy cushions in the front row tangled feet with the band. Joe was one of the fortunate who'd snagged a chair. He sat against the wall, his body moving like a bag of bones to the jaunty, brass-heavy Dixieland jazz. Eleanor appeared at his feet.

"Promise me," her lips said through the trumpet solo. "Promise me we'll never fight again."

A month later, Katrina hit. Eleanor picked up the phone. Ivy answered. The fight outside Leah's Pralines was never spoken of again.

The phone calls with Ivy grew more cordial and less frequent. Ivy had gotten a job as a docent at a local museum. After unsuccessful back surgery, Mary Marge was put down. John-Tyler had three birthdays. Eleanor dutifully sent what Ivy instructed.

Late one night, the phone rang, a 504 number. It was Lester, from a New Orleans hotel. He'd spent the day with Bucky and Ivy.

"That night of my party," Lester said. "In New York. When Ivy went back to his hotel. I knew then it was all over for you."

"Why are you saying this?" Eleanor asked. "What happened?"

"When was the last time you saw them?"

It had been three years.

"Why?" Eleanor said, panic seizing her chest. "What happened?"

"Don't you see?" Lester said, drunk and not making sense. "He's trying to plant your fingerprints on his crime scene."

Eleanor called Ivy the next day and asked how she was. How she *really* was. Ivy gave an unexpected answer: on pills.

"Drugs?" Eleanor asked.

"Medication," Ivy corrected. "Eleanor, it changes everything! In the past, something little would happen, like Taffy screwing the lid too tight on the raspberry jam. I'd try tapping it on the counter, running it under hot water and John-Tyler would be asking, 'Why are you crying, Mama?' And I'd think, I can't even open a jar of jam without my misery rippling out into the world. But now that I'm on medication, it's a jar of jam! I'll eat my toast with cinnamon sugar! What a strange product of the modern age I've become. They should make a movie about it. A medicated woman going through her day with normal reactions to ordinary life and at her side is her former self who completely breaks down at the very same things."

"Gwyneth Paltrow can play both parts," Eleanor said flatly.

"See, there's an example," Ivy said. "The old me would have burst into tears because *I'm* an actress. *I* should play both parts. But the improved me? I think, yes, Gwyneth Paltrow would also be wonderful in the role."

Matthew Flood died of liver failure at the age of sixty-six. He'd been sober for a decade. The lady from Dallas in whose guesthouse Matty and the girls had lived couldn't make it to the memorial service. But she'd arranged for a convoy of red Jeeps to meet the mourners at Wagner Park and four-wheel them to the top of Aspen Highlands. There, they'd scatter Matty's ashes on his favorite run, the Moment of Truth.

A dozen of Matty's AA friends, joined by Ivy, Eleanor, and Joe, zigzagged their way up the snowcat roads through the spring slush and arrived at the picnic bench that had been there forever. Welcoming them was an orange-and-blue Broncos wreath, barbecue from the Hickory House, and the Bobby Mason Band playing Matty's favorite song, "Please Come to Boston." The lady from Dallas had remained mysterious but loyal to the end.

There was champagne for fifty but Ivy was the only one drinking.

To Eleanor, these friends of Matty's were graciously free of judgment toward the two daughters who never visited. Joe wept upon seeing the canister of ashes on the bed of white Aspen branches sprouting with lime-colored buds; Eleanor felt nothing.

It was the early death of her mother that had taught Eleanor to shut herself off. Deep down Eleanor knew she must have been born a warmer soul. She wasn't meant to be so self-reliant. One day, Matty had forgotten to pick up the girls at day camp and they'd had to walk the five miles from the T-Lazy-7 Ranch. Matty came home after the bars closed and realized what he'd done. He crawled into Eleanor's twin bed and cried. "I'm weak," he said. "You're so much better than I can ever be." The snow from Matty's hiking boots melted dirt on Eleanor's Life Savers sheets.

"You okay?" Joe took Eleanor's hand as they settled into chairs to share memories of Matty.

"I'm crazy about you, Joe," Eleanor whispered.

A woman with a weathered face and a Tyrolean sweater launched into a story. "Of course there was the time Matty brought that goat into the Jerome Bar!"

Amid the appreciative chuckles, Ivy muttered ominously, "He was a useless bastard."

Eleanor had heard it, but the woman hadn't. She continued. "I think he won it off Jim Salter."

"Jim Salter had a pony, not a goat!" former mayor Bill Stirling said, laughing. "But I'll tell you who did have a goat—"

"He was a drunk and a bookie," Ivy growled. "He left us alone for weeks at a time to fend for ourselves."

The attention now turned to Ivy, but her unfocused eyes rested on a tuft of grass a foot from the tin of ashes. She held a tippy champagne glass. On the dirt at her side, her own personal bottle.

Ivy raised her head and addressed the dumbfounded gray-haired woman. "We ate food off drugstore shelves."

"I didn't mean—"

"He didn't know what grade I was in," Ivy said, leaning forward. "My teeth were loose in my head from lack of nutrition. He let me become pen pals with prisoners from the back of *Rolling Stone* magazine. I'm sorry if I don't see what's so hilarious about bringing a goat into the Jerome Bar."

Eleanor touched Ivy's arm, but she kept going, now addressing the group.

"And because your beloved Matty paid no attention to me, I

had to go marry a guy who controls my every move. Now look at me." Ivy stood up, her chair flipping back into the fine dirt with a poof. "Know why I look like this?"

Eleanor and Joe had wondered. Ivy had arrived dressed in a long-sleeved shirt and an ankle-length silk skirt, her hip bones pointing through like headlights. Her hair was an unflattering red that picked up her rashy complexion.

"Hair dye has toxins that will hurt the fetus if I ever get pregnant again, so Bucky makes me use henna. He thinks I throw myself at every man I come across the way I did at him the night we met. And at you too, Joe, the day of my wedding. Now I can only go out if I'm covered from ankle to wrist like an Orthodox Jew!"

Even this group, desensitized to tales of shocking behavior, shifted in their chairs at the grace note of anti-Semitism.

"My whole life," Ivy said, now beginning to cry, "no matter how gutter-bad things got, at least I was better off than Matty."

Eleanor stood up. Ivy moved away. "But look at me!" Ivy yanked her arm back, even though no one had reached for it. "Like father, like daughter, second-class citizens, there at the whim of the people in the big house!"

"I know, Ivy." Eleanor moved toward her sister, but Ivy ran off and shouted the rest from twenty feet away, like a hostage taker.

"If I leave, Bucky will get full custody of John-Tyler! Bucky's drooling at the prospect of a court battle. His family owns every judge in New Orleans. He claims he was sold a bill of defective goods. He says you and Joe pulled a fast one by dumping your trash on his rich family, like I'm the crazy lady in the attic."

Joe came up from behind and took Ivy by the upper arms. The strength of his grip made her go limp. He hustled her into a Jeep, borrowed the keys from the driver, and told Eleanor he'd meet her back at the hotel.

As Joe drove, Ivy kept her face turned away. Her only movement was to grip the roll bar tightly anytime the Jeep tipped down a steep switchback. When they got off the mountain and onto the pavement of Maroon Creek Road, Ivy finally spoke.

"I'm sure you're wondering what's happened to me," she said without looking over. "I am too."

Joe drove to the campus of the ritzy Aspen Institute with its Buckminster Fuller dome and sculptures by Herbert Bayer and Andy Goldsworthy. Joe parked the Jeep. He and Ivy walked along a path leading to the music tent. They passed manicured emerald mounds, some ten feet high. A woman in a down vest stood at the top of one, playing King of the Mountain with her Westie. At the edge of the lawn, cut through the sagebrush, a hidden path known only to locals. It led to an arc of benches tucked inside an aspen grove. This was where Eleanor and Ivy would go as children. This was their favorite spot.

Ivy sat down, home again.

"I'm validating everything you said," Joe said. "We'll figure this out the same way we've figured everything else out."

"You were crying up there," Ivy said.

"Mortality and nature," Joe said. "It gets me every time. You try your best, or you don't try your best. The mountains don't care."

"Gee," Ivy said.

Joe laughed. "I'm sorry."

Ivy snapped a sagebrush twig and rubbed the leaves into her fingertips. She held them up for Joe to smell.

Joe leaned in. Ivy touched his face. He pulled away.

"I don't think I drank enough water when I got here," Ivy said.

"We're at eight thousand feet," Joe said. "Eleven on the mountain."

"Would you mind getting me some?" Ivy asked.

"When I get back, we can talk about everything. I want to listen."

Joe walked the fifty yards to the music tent. It was May; the place was desolate. In an unlocked concession stand he dug out a stack of paper cups. He pulled off four, found a men's room, and filled them with chilly tap water.

Joe made his way back to the secret spot, careful not to spill a drop of his offering.

He arrived at the circle. The benches were bare.

Joe emerged from the aspen grove. He saw no sign of Ivy. The woman and her dog were gone. Joe sensed another absence. The patch of red. The Jeep. He'd left the keys on the floor.

Joe stomped down Highway 82 toward town. It had begun to rain. The tops of the mountains were sugar-dusted with snow.

The jolly convoy of Jeeps cruised by on their way back from the memorial. One skidded to a stop. It was Eleanor.

"That was the last time," Joe said. "Do you hear me? I'm done with her."

They returned to the Limelight Hotel. Ivy's room was empty, her bags gone. Eleanor received a call. The missing Jeep had turned up at the Aspen airport, parked in a fire lane, engine running.

A few months before the memorial, Eleanor and Joe had decided it was time for Eleanor to go off the pill. The morning of the service, on the way to Wagner Park, sudden nausea had her retching into a wine barrel spilling with the twisted brown of last year's petunias. She wrote it off as the thin air.

The next day, on her way back to Seattle, in the women's room at the Denver airport, Eleanor coughed up bile.

"Are you all right?" Joe asked when she emerged.

"Fine," Eleanor said. "Just a long line."

Joe wasn't continuing to Seattle with his wife but flying from Denver to Nairobi. He was already a day late to meet two other doctors for pro bono surgeries. He'd been raising money and making arrangements for the past year.

If Joe thought Eleanor might be pregnant, she knew he'd cancel his trip. She kissed him good-bye at his gate and hoped to have good news to spring on him when he returned.

Back in Seattle, the good news came in the form of a fierce underwater heartbeat and an ultrasound printed on delicate thermal paper. The baby would arrive around Thanksgiving. But, as Dr. Koo had said, Eleanor was forty and just eight weeks into her first pregnancy. "Best not get ahead of ourselves."

On her way out of the doctor's office, Eleanor received a call from Ivy.

"It's over," Ivy said. "I'm leaving him."

For the next week, whenever Ivy could break free from Bucky—at the market, at the playground, in her parked car while she pretended to be at the gym—she'd share stories of his tempestuous jealousy and histrionics.

It wasn't the end of Bucky that had Eleanor living in Technicolor. It was being a sister again. There was no relief deeper than being loved by the person who'd known you the longest. Eleanor's heart giggled with mad abundance: so much to share, so much goodwill, so many notes to compare, so many ways to help and be helped. She went out into the world, everything a performance for her coconspirator, Ivy. It was Eleanor at her vibrant best.

"Oh, Eleanor," Ivy sighed while Bucky was off getting takeout. "I lost myself and threw you out in the confusion. How can you not hate me?"

"All that matters is we're back."

They both recognized that Bucky would never let Ivy just walk away. So the sisters hatched a plan. While Bucky was receiving an honor from the city for hiring good-behavior prisoners to pull the Khaos float, Ivy would whisk John-Tyler to the airport. Eleanor had two plane tickets paid for and waiting. She'd found a divorce lawyer. She'd put down first and last month's rent on a town house in West Seattle. Ivy could work in Joe's office.

Ivy found it hard to believe Joe would approve. "He can't be much of a fan after what I did to him in Aspen."

"Joe is totally on board," Eleanor said.

Joe wasn't on board. Joe was in Africa without phone or Internet.

It was madness, the collision course Eleanor had set in motion. Her imagination became a battleground of incoming fire from Ivy and Joe.

Ivy: But Eleanor, without a good lawyer I'll lose custody of my son!

Joe: Me bankrolling a custody battle between Ivy and Bucky, are you kidding?

Ivy: Don't you have your own money from *Looper Wash*?

Joe: When I make money, it's "our" money, but when you make money, it's "your" money?

Ivy: Joe has never understood what you and I are to each other.

Joe: I have six siblings. And no drama. It's called boundaries.

Ivy: I promise to pay you back when I win my settlement.

Joe: We both know Bucky will never give your sister a dime.

Ivy: I can work it off by being your nanny.

Joe: An insane child helping us with the baby? I don't think so.

Ivy: What matters is we beat this guy.

Joe: Nobody beats the Troubled Troubadour.

And then horns would honk and Eleanor would snap to. She'd been sitting at a green light.

Ivy's plane landed at noon. Eleanor bought a car seat and decorated the back of an envelope. *Welcome to Seattle, Ivy and J.T.!* She stood in the baggage claim among the limo drivers and watched.

Ivy emerged wearing a sleeveless shift, her hair blond again.

"Yay!" said Eleanor.

John-Tyler wasn't at her side. Eleanor's eyes went to the next wedge of the revolving door. A little boy in a navy blazer emerged, holding hands with his father, Bucky.

They stood there, facing Eleanor, the three of them.

"This was my choice," Ivy said. "It has nothing to do with Bucky. The IVF and the pills were making me overly emotional. I needed help, I see that now. And I'm getting it."

John-Tyler, in Gucci loafers you could fit in your palm, was his own little person. He held a plastic dinosaur and had Bucky's chin. Eleanor wouldn't have known Bucky had a chin until she saw it on Ivy's son.

Without a word, Bucky handed Eleanor a list of conditions. She scanned it numbly. If she wanted to visit Ivy, she could come to

New Orleans and stay in a hotel. She wouldn't be allowed in the house. She was never to be left alone with John-Tyler.

Eleanor ransacked Ivy's face for the slightest something: a held-back tear, a desperate flash in the eye saying *I'll call you later*, a quivering lip. But nothing.

Bucky held out a Neiman Marcus shopping bag. "We won't be needing this."

In it a slab of leather. On its spine, THE FLOOD GIRLS. The shock of it, and of Ivy's acquiescence, paralyzed Eleanor.

Bucky, without lowering his hand, let go of the bag. It dropped to the floor with an unremarkable thud.

"Let's go find the departure level, shall we?" Bucky said, his arm now around Ivy's waist. "Our plane leaves in an hour and I fear the powers that be will make us once again endure security."

"Yes, my love."

Bucky turned to Eleanor. "You blame me, of course. One day you will understand this is entirely your doing. You never gave me a chance. Yes, I do live a smallish life in New Orleans. And one might say I'm overinvested in Carnival. But I'm ferociously loyal to my family, you see. Any hardships I have with your sister are a function of me wanting the best for her and our son. I'm the first to admit that Ivy and I have had difficulties in our marriage. What couple hasn't? But it's basic emotional intelligence that when someone comes to you with their one-sided horror stories, you listen. You don't plot their divorce. It's true, Eleanor, you and I possess different styles. Last time I checked, the world allowed for such things. There's a Buddhist proverb: 'Just because a raft helps you cross the river, you need not carry that raft on your back for the rest of your life.' In other words, Eleanor, you're the raft, and Ivy has decided to put you down."

And then it was three backs walking away.

It took several seconds for Eleanor to speak.

"Where are the derringers?" she found herself screaming as she charged them. "I want my guns! I want my guns back!"

Ten minutes later, Eleanor was in the back of a police car outside baggage claim. She explained to the young cop it had been a family argument and that the guns were darling antiques that didn't fire, practically metaphors. Even if they did fire, they were mounted on a wall in another state.

"You've got to calm down, ma'am." It was the cop, through a crack in the window. "I don't want to take you downtown. But you really gotta chill here."

Please God, don't let all this toxic fear and rage hurt the baby. Please don't let Joe get back from Kenya and find out I got arrested. I promise you, God, if you get me out of here with a healthy baby and without Joe knowing, Joe and the baby will be my family. I'll never think about Bucky and Ivy again.

"Get it together, ma'am. Count to three and put it behind you. Ready?"

"One, two, three."

Right after Timby was born, that's when it was toughest not to have a sister. Breast-feeding. Sleep schedules. Eleanor had found a baby class whose instructor believed high chairs, slings, and tummy time were bad, even bordered on child abuse, and of course Eleanor wanted to compare notes with her sister, a mother before her. Everyday life was booby-trapped with reminders. (Blueberries: the time Eleanor and Ivy had made cold blueberry soup from *The*

Silver Palate Cookbook at their walk-up on Bank Street and it stained the guests' teeth purple.) But as soon as a memory of Ivy was triggered, Eleanor snapped a rubber band around her wrist. If she didn't have a rubber band, she scolded herself out loud: "No!"

When Eleanor had gotten back from the airport, after the nice cop let her drive herself home, she stripped the apartment of all things Ivy. (Kidney beans: when they lived in New York, they decided to throw a chili party, and because the kitchen was so tiny, they'd cooked the beans the night before but left them out, causing them to ferment, and they'd ended up having to order takeout from Empire Szechuan.) Eleanor cleansed her closet of all clothes reminding her of Ivy. A Fiorucci T-shirt washed a thousand times and soft as silk went to Goodwill. The Conran apron, it would have been bought on Astor Place during the Bank Street days. That went too.

Books. *Jane Eyre* went. *The Drama of the Gifted Child* with Ivy's underlining. *Lonesome Dove,* torn in half on a camping trip so they could read it at the same time, then duct-taped back together. A *Vanity Fair* with Daryl Hannah on the cover and Ivy's Dior ad inside. Shoe boxes of photos, ones Eleanor had been meaning to put into albums: any with Ivy went in the trash, and the trash went down the chute.

The Flood Girls kept looking back at her.

Years before, Joyce Primm, a young book editor, had expressed interest in Eleanor's expanding the illustrations into a graphic memoir. Eleanor had demurred.

But what if she did get them published...?

What if she did flesh out the story of their childhood? The tale of losing her beloved mother and becoming a mother to Ivy at age nine. There were a thousand moments that called to her! The time she and Ivy told Matty they were going to explore the Midnight Mine and he'd barely looked up from the paper to say, "Nice knowing you." Or when Tess, after her diagnosis, could be found sitting in her parked car, listening over and over to "Frank Mills" from the *Hair* eight-track.

Eleanor's imagination lit up the sky with scenarios of Bucky wandering into a Garden District bookstore and seeing *The Flood Girls* as a graphic memoir. The injury! The humiliation! The panicked buying-up of all copies in New Orleans so nobody would see it! She could finally outflank him! People telling Ivy, "I had no idea what a terrible childhood you had. Thank God you and your sister have each other." And Ivy would have to lie or admit that she'd thrown Eleanor away like trash. Either way, sweet vengeance!

Yes, Eleanor had drawn those twelve illustrations out of love. But that didn't mean she couldn't weaponize them.

Charming Joyce Primm into a book deal over drinks at the W Hotel made Eleanor feel both unhinged and exhilarated, like a woman throwing all her boyfriend's clothes onto the front lawn.

But when it came time to sit down and write the memoir, the vindictive energy was gone. Eleanor tried to recapture it for art's sake but couldn't. She shoved *The Flood Girls* in the back of a closet to be dealt with later.

Eight years passed.

The reminders of Ivy would always be there. Depending on the day, they made Eleanor feel angry, wistful, devastated, or nothing at all. Eleanor couldn't *not* be reminded of Ivy. But she could control the recovery time. After so many years of practice, it now took Eleanor no more than five minutes to bounce back.

Just last weekend, Eleanor, Joe, and Timby had gone to an inn on Lummi Island. It had a cool dark library with a treasure box of tea bags, and newspapers on wooden rods. Perfect for an early October afternoon while Timby and Joe kayaked. Eleanor would read the *New York Times* the way it was meant to be read, leisurely, from first page to last. She wouldn't even skip the obituaries.

There was a woman who'd made one fortune importing bananas from the Caribbean and a second fortune growing cotton. It sounded vaguely familiar. Eleanor revisited the headline.

ARMANITO TRUMBO CHARBONNEAU

PILLAR OF NEW ORLEANS SOCIETY

DEAD AT 92

Before Eleanor could stop them, her eyes dropped to the last line.

"She is survived by grandson Barnaby Fanning, the historian, and his two children, John-Tyler and Delphine."

Blur

"Put something under her head," someone was saying.

I opened my eyes to a halo of concern. Spencer, Timby, a museum guard, and a stylish older woman knelt over me, the woman unspooling a long floral scarf from her neck. She folded the scarf in half and in half again and again until it was the size of a head. My head, it turned out. I dutifully raised it and she placed her scarf underneath. A downside of extremely fine cashmere? Despite how many times it's folded, it has the cushioning capacity of typing paper.

From a secondary arc of standing people: "I called an ambulance."

"For me?" I said. "I don't need an ambulance." Although I did feel a bit foggy...

"Just relax and breathe," said the lady in charge...the museum director? She must have been eighty, with her pinched skin, density of crags, and white hair, curly and flying. Giant black-rimmed glasses dwarfed her small face, defiantly free of makeup.

"Do you see her pupils?" someone whispered.

"Mama!" Timby threw himself across me.

"Please!" I patted his back. "I'm fine."

A person off to the side excitedly recounted the incident. "I'm just checking my stocks and I see this woman running, and *wham*, next thing I know, she's on the ground."

"Get up," Timby said.

"Yeah," someone said. "She's not getting up."

"If you're talking about me," I said to them around Timby's head, "it's because I'm choosing not to get up."

"Do you need some water?" an installer asked.

"Nah."

He turned to Timby. "Do you need some water?"

"Is it VitaminWater?"

"Someone should call a loved one," said an excited woman. "Little boy, do you have a father?"

"Of course he has a father," I said. "What do you think this is?"

"Do we know how to reach him?"

"The number's on her phone," Timby said.

"Eleanor?" Spencer came in. "May we borrow your phone?"

"I dropped it in a bait bucket."

A collective "Hunh?"

"It had stopped serving me."

"Wow," said Spencer, and "Wow!" again, the second time spread across three syllables.

"Wow what?" the museum director asked Spencer, for which I was grateful, because it meant I didn't have to.

"Sometimes she says things," he clarified...kind of.

"Is she always like this?" asked someone who was met by a round of shrugs. This crowd was sure easy to stump.

"Remind me never to go on *Family Feud* with you people," I said.

A huddle had formed near a hulking green sculpture.

"Did it always have this dent in it?" came a voice.

"Dent?" Spencer spun around to look.

"You can go," I told him, because it seemed like that's what he wanted. "I release you."

Spencer bolted to the sculpture. Now the museum director was craning her neck to see.

"You can go too," I told her. "Everyone who wants to go, go."

The museum director and the installer scampered over, leaving just me and Timby.

I stroked his hair. "How are you, darling?"

"I wish you'd get up."

"Then I'll get up." I sat up. "Are you happy now?"

"All the way up," he said, tugging my arm.

"This steel is an eighth of an inch thick," said someone near the sculpture. "Look at the dent she put in it."

They all turned to me with grudging admiration.

"Brett Favre!" I announced triumphantly.

"Lie back down," said Spencer.

"Brett Favre is the quarterback I couldn't remember, the one with the thumb."

"That's really good," Spencer said. "Just lie down."

"Don't," Timby threatened.

"If you forget a name and you can't recall it," I told Spencer, "it could be early-onset Alzheimer's. But if it pops into your head later, you're good."

"I've heard that too," said the museum director.

She had perfect posture. That's the way I was going to age. Let everything go, but dress with flair and stand up straight. "Living out loud" they call it, unless that's something different. And those giant black glasses: I'm definitely going to go that route. Like Elaine Stritch. Or Frances Lear. Or Iris Apfel. Where were these names even coming from? I was on fire with useless references!

"Go when you can, not when you need to," I said.

They all looked at me.

"Advice about going to the bathroom," I said. "Sound advice."

Writing me off completely, they returned to their panicky huddle.

"We're covered," the museum director explained to someone quietly. "We have liability."

"For the show," said the blue hands. "But the show hasn't started yet."

"That's not how insurance works," the museum director spit back.

"I'd put my money on her," I called over. "With age comes wisdom."

Spencer narrowed his eyes at me. The worry patrol situated themselves so I could see only backs.

On the floor. My purse. The set of keys.

D-E-L-P-H-I-N-E.

Oh God.

"Come," I whispered to Timby. I grabbed the keys and stood up. My head was lead and positioned wrong on my neck. I blinked a couple of times, righting my center of gravity. "See?"

Timby's answer was drowned out by an approaching siren.

Spencer and the rest were too absorbed in their whisper-fight to notice us slip out.

Aw, Spencer, poor Spencer. I hoped he'd find success one day.

Oh, wait...

The only sign of life as we headed up the Galer Street steps was a bunny hopping around the front lawn.

"Aww," said Timby.

"Where is everyone?" I asked.

"Raking leaves out back."

"The whole school?"

"With our homeless buddies," he said.

An empty school! This played perfectly into my gutless plan: to slip in without anyone seeing, return the keys, and slip out.

What I had done was truly unforgivable. Because of me, some young mom had spent the day half out of her mind searching for her keys. I don't care how thin or pleased with yourself you are, nobody deserves that.

As for why I couldn't just admit that I had to learn from the goddamned newspaper that my sister has a daughter, so in a *farkakte* attempt to get back at her, I stole the keys of a woman with a daughter of the same name...

Would you?

The whole thing left me badly shaken. In the past, I'd often been called crazy. But it was endearing-crazy, kooky-crazy, we're-all-a-little-crazy-crazy. Stealing that young mom's keys? Even The Trick couldn't spin that into anything other than scary-crazy.

I tugged open the front door and crossed through the foyer.

The conference room was dark; the table still had an enticing cornucopia of spots in which to tuck the keys and scram. I grabbed the doorknob. Locked!

" 'Happy birthday to you...' " filtered through the hallways.

I followed the voices into the administration suite. The outer office, Lila's area, was empty.

" 'Happy birthday, dear Gwen-sie! Happy birthday to you!' "

They were all in Gwen's office having cake. Perfect! I reached over Lila's counter and plucked a Sharpie out of her cup. I grabbed an envelope and, in big block letters, wrote, FOUND THESE.

But then, a voice...a loud voice...a voice in the same room with me: "I'll get a knife!"

It was Stesha, the afterschool coordinator.

"Hi, Eleanor!" Stesha did what she always did when she saw me: rolled up her T-shirt to show off her *Looper Wash* tattoo. She was a Vivian apparently.

"There it is!" I said. Because what can you say?

"Do you need Lila?" Stesha asked.

"No, no—"

"Oh, hello." Lila now! "How's Timby feeling?"

"Much better."

The three of us stood there.

"Can we help you with something?" Lila asked.

"I wanted to sign out," I said. "I forgot to this morning. And didn't you send an e-mail reminding everyone to sign out if they left early? Citizenship or something?"

"Oh, you didn't have to make a special trip," Lila said. "I was here when you picked up Timby."

"That's just for parents who take their kids directly out of the classroom," Stesha clarified.

The whorl of dull information had a mysterious, paralyzing effect.

"Is that for me?" Lila finally said of the envelope in my hand.

"Nope!" I said, ripping it to pieces.

"Tell Timby we hope he feels better."

I went out to the hallway where my son was kneeling, his face close to a padlocked Lucite box filled with dollar bills.

"Mom, look! There must be a thousand dollars in here!"

Above the box, a sign: DOLLAR DROP. Beside that, a Post-it note. LAST DAY TO GIVE!

"It's to buy socks and blankets for a homeless shelter," Timby said.

"Sheesh," I said. "Homeless I get. I just don't know why it has to be all homeless all the time."

"The parents are counting the money today," Timby said. "If Galer Street beats the other schools, we get to go to Wild Waves."

The lights now blazed in the conference room. Two young moms and one young dad were on hand (the same ones? You're asking *me?*) clearing space on the table for the counting party. (Galer Street's policy: If a job requires two volunteers, why not send out harassing e-mails asking for six?)

It gave me an idea.

"Timby, go to your locker and get your backpack."

"I have my backpack."

"Get your gym shoes."

"Why?"

"So we can wash them."

"How do you wash gym shoes?"

"In the washing machine."

Timby made a face. "You do not."

"I'm not having this conversation," I said. "Go."

Timby trudged up the staircase to his locker.

The fifth-graders' Lewis and Clark journals lined the wall. Feigning interest, I took the keys from my purse and slipped them into the dollar drop. They hardly made a sound, that's how many dollars these do-gooders had dropped.

In minutes, one of those parent volunteers would open the box, find the keys, and return them to Delphine's mom. No harm, no foul...ish.

Through the second-grade classroom window I could see the school yard. Wee ones carrying rakes formed into columns, preparing to come inside.

Time to scram. I fished in my purse for my car keys. They felt funny. I looked down.

D-E-L-P-H-I-N-E.

Gah! I spun around.

My keys! In the dollar drop! The *padlocked* dollar drop!

A flashback to the days when I belonged to the New York Health and Racquet Club. They'd been experiencing a rash of locker break-ins; it turned out a bad element had been popping open the padlocks. How? By slipping a gym towel through the loop, holding both ends, and yanking down really hard. I'd always wanted to give it a whirl.

Farther down the Lewis and Clark wall, the kids had hung tomahawks: sticks and stones tied together with...leather strips!

And they say God doesn't provide.

I unwound the leather from a tomahawk and folded it back and forth a few times.

The coast was still clear, but the kids were now on the march. In a minute they'd burst in.

I threaded the leather through the loop in the lock and got a firm grip on both ends. I gave a sharp tug, and...

The box flipped off the table and crashed to the floor!

I dropped to my knees. The goddamned box was still locked. I grabbed another tomahawk and began pummeling the lock. The stupid thing wouldn't give up the ghost. Finally, the hinge screws popped free. I pried off the lid and reached in, dollar bills splashing everywhere. I grabbed my keys, jumped up, and threw *D-E-L-P-H-I-N-E* onto the money spill. Success! And nobody saw me.

Except Timby, standing there holding his dirty sneakers.

"Have you ever heard of the word *subconscious?*" I asked Timby in the mirror as my car tipped down Queen Anne Hill.

"No."

"Your subconscious is a hidden part of you that does things you don't realize and thinks things you're not fully aware of."

"Oh." Timby's head was turned; he was looking out the window.

"It's almost as if there's a separate person inside of you who has ideas all their own. And often those ideas aren't good ideas."

Timby twisted his mouth. The rush of brick apartment buildings still held his gaze.

"I guess what I'm trying to say is, this morning, *a part of me* grabbed Delphine's mom's keys."

"Your hand."

I readjusted the mirror.

"What do you want to do when we get home?" I asked. "Play Rat-a-Tat Cat? Make pizza? We can watch *I Know, Right?*"

"Can I watch it by myself?"

We stopped at a light outside the Key Arena. A half dozen monks with shaved heads, wearing saffron robes and those cloth shoulder bags you make in Sewing 101, crossed in front of us. On another corner, pedestrians with a DON'T WALK sign waited even though no cars were coming.

"Seattle," I said. "I've never seen a city of pedestrians less invested in crossing the street."

"Maybe they're just happy," Timby said.

I passed the gift basket back. "Tear into that thing, will you?"

With a frightening single-mindedness, Timby tried sliding off the bow, but it only tightened. He pulled at the ends, but the knot was glued. He clawed at open folds in the cellophane but could only jab a finger in. Finally, he grabbed a pencil out of the cup holder and viciously stabbed at the wrapper.

"Gee," I said. "Nice follow-through."

The monks reached a food truck and stood in line. On the hood was a chrome snout. PIG 'N' SHIT it said.

"You know what might be fun to watch together?" I said. "*Looper Wash*."

"Kate O. watches *Looper Wash*," Timby said, biting into an olive roll. "Her moms have the DVDs. It's their favorite show."

I pulled into our alley and clicked open the garage.

"What does it even mean?" Timby asked. "*Looper Wash?*"

"The woman who wrote the pilot had four daughters."

"Violet Parry," Timby said. "She's your best friend."

"That's right. The oldest was hers and the rest were adopted from Ethiopia, Cambodia, and somewhere else."

"If they're adopted, they're hers too," Timby corrected.

I glided into our space and turned off the engine. "Violet wrote a pilot about four girls who hang out in a wash in a town called Looper. *Looper Wash*."

"What's a wash?" he asked.

"A dry riverbed." I adjusted the mirror so we could see each other. "I know, it's kind of weird. You always need to explain it. The girls are hilarious. They hate technology and progress. And hippies and food waste."

Timby, eating cookies now, looked unconvinced.

"Trust me," I said. "It's funny."

"It sounds mean."

"When you get older, mean is funny." I turned around. "Because Violet and I were women doing a show that both adults and children loved, that was full of social satire and girl power—it was just a really big deal." I turned to face the front.

"Are you crying?" Timby asked.

I opened the door and got out.

"We don't have to watch it if you don't want," Timby said, still cradling the gift basket, now a hangover of raffia grass, empty wrappers, open jars, and loose Dutch mints.

"I do want," I said. We got into the elevator. I pushed *L* and the doors sealed us in.

"Let's start with the pilot," I said. "It's a little slow, but there are funny things to watch for."

"Like what?"

The doors opened and we rounded the corner to the mailboxes.

"The show was hand-colored in Hungary..." I opened the mailbox. Junk, junk, junk. "And the script had the girls feeding their ponies Junior Mints."

"Really?"

"We had a guy on staff who claimed ponies love Junior Mints—"

A large envelope from Jazz Alley. SEASON TICKETS INSIDE. Despite my protestations, Joe must have re-subscribed. At least he heeded my pleas and seemed to have chosen only a couple of shows.

"Anyway," I said to Timby, tucking the tickets under my arm, "in Hungary they got our designs but I guess they weren't familiar with Junior Mints and decided they were a type of meat."

Timby hung on my every word.

"We didn't have time to correct it," I said. "It goes by quickly, but if you slow it down, you can see Millicent feeding her pony bloody hunks of meat."

"I want to see that!" Timby said.

Suddenly, a cry from across the lobby.

"There she is!"

Sydney Madsen! Rushing at me with her skinny runner's body and weird water shoes.

I gasped, realizing.

Ajay the doorman was by her side. Whatever Sydney Madsen had just put him through, it was above his pay grade.

"Eleanor, you're okay!" Sydney grabbed my arms and shook me. "What is going on?"

"I totally messed up! I thought we were having lunch."

"Which I gathered from the number of voice-mail messages you left." It took twice as long to say as a normal person due to her plodding enunciation. "My phone was turned off because I was in a two-and-a-half-hour conference. When I came out, there were five messages from you."

At water parks, certain rides have a sign: YOU *WILL* GET WET. Sydney should have to wear a sign: YOU *WILL* GET BORED.

"I feel so stupid," I said. "I'm totally fine."

But Sydney Madsen wasn't done. "I tried calling your cell phone but there was no answer. I tried calling your house. I called the restaurant. I came here and this young man let me up to your floor to knock on your door but he wouldn't let me into your apartment. I called Joe's office and they said he was on vacation."

"She hit her head," Timby chimed in. "In the museum. She passed out. She threw away her phone."

Sydney brushed aside my bangs and looked startled. I raised my hand to my forehead.

"Ooh," I said with a flinch. A goose egg had formed.

"Have you gone to the hospital?" Sydney asked.

"I'll be fine," I said. "Let me go upstairs and lie down."

"That's exactly what you don't do," she said. "Eleanor, there's a concussion protocol. Have you tested yourself with the concussion app?"

"There's a concussion app?" Timby asked.

"Wait," Sydney said. "Please tell me you have not been driving with a head injury."

"Umm," Timby said, smiling adorably.

"I've held my tongue for years," Sydney said, off on another slow, insistent tear. "But I'm concerned enough by your pattern of behavior to say it now: you must start taking some agency over your life."

Is there anything more joy-killing than hearing *agency* in that context? Consider yourself warned. Say *agency* all you want, just know you won't be hanging out with me.

"You're walking around half in this world and half who knows where," Sydney droned on. "I'm a busy person. I canceled an appointment so I could come find you. I walked up and down the parking garage looking for your car. I saw Joe's but not yours. I was sick with worry. It's almost as if you have zero consideration for others."

"She got you this." Timby handed Sydney the ravaged gift basket with its ripped cellophane and half-devoured food items.

"I'm taking you to the hospital." Sydney held out her palm. "You're not driving."

"Okay." I handed her my car keys. "I'll go."

"You will?" asked Timby.

"Let me run upstairs and get my insurance card. I'll be right down. Come on, Timby."

Up in our apartment, I went straight to the utility closet. I pulled the top off the vintage flour canister where we kept our extra keys.

"Mom, what are you doing?"

"Something fun."

Back in the elevator, Timby reached for *L*. I stopped him just in time. I pushed *P2*.

"Sydney said she saw Dad's car," I explained. "If it's true, that's a significant development."

"It is?"

Timby followed me into the garage.

Sure enough, Joe's car sat in his space. He parks one level down from me (don't you love him, giving me the better parking space!), which is why I hadn't noticed it on our way in. I used his spare key to unlock the doors.

"Are we getting in?" Timby asked.

I started the engine and waited for the display to boot up. The speakers blared inane jam-band music from the Sirius channel Joe likes.

"Yech," I said, slapping it off. "A live concert needs to be listened to live. Otherwise, it's like eating day-old salad."

Timby hooted with laughter from the backseat.

"What?" I asked.

"Day-old salad! That's hilarious!"

"Gee," I said. "I always thought you didn't get my jokes."

"I get them," he said. "Most of the time they're just not funny."

Our neighborhood appeared on the GPS. I cycled through the menu options until I found TRACE ROUTE.

On the screen, our neighborhood again, but this time overlaid with dotted lines showing the routes Joe had driven. I zoomed out to get a sense of Joe's big picture.

The thickest line formed between our apartment and his office. But there was another line, nearly as fat, between our apartment and a mystery destination about five miles away. In Magnolia, a sleepy neighborhood on a hill where we never went. Where there was no reason to go.

"What are you doing?" asked Timby.

I zoomed in. A residential neighborhood. Not good.

"Get in," I said. "Seat belt on."

We screeched up the parking-garage spiral and into traffic. I couldn't resist a peek. In the lobby, Sydney Madsen had her back to us, talking with flapping arms to poor Ajay. His eyes widened when he realized it was me and Timby smoking up Third Avenue.

"You know how I said your subconscious is a deep-down part of you that sometimes has bad ideas?" I said to Timby. "This isn't that. This is me, your mom, doing something I know full well is a bad idea."

Following the trail of electronic bread crumbs, I rounded the corner north onto Denny Avenue. The sun seared my eyes. I frantically lowered the visor. A photo fell out. The three of us, last year, petting angora rabbits at the state fair in Puyallup. A wave of unease: happiness in retrospect.

"Aww," Timby said. "Can I see?"

I passed the photo over my shoulder.

Right after Joe and I moved to Seattle, we went to the state fair, my first one ever. It has since become a tradition. Of course this native New Yorker was horrified at the parolee vibe and average weight of my fellow milling attendees. Around every corner, teardrop trailers sold raspberry scones. PRIDE OF WASHINGTON, the signs beamed. I thought, How sad for Washington State, to be so proud over so little.

Such could be said of the entertainment offered. We were expected to marvel over goats in pens, be amazed at vegetables arranged to look like the Washington State flag, gather around for jewelry-cleaning demos. I must have been on my feet too long, or maybe it was the September heat, but when I saw the genuine delight Joe took in cheering his entry in a pig race ("Look at that! They're chasing an Oreo!"), my defenses went kaput. I actually felt at one with the doughy white mass of humanity, these Washingtonians with their guns and Jesus and BluBlockers.

And I thought, How sad for *you*, New York City, you self-absorbed *crack whore, with your status-obsessed, edgy, darting eyes, your* choked sidewalks, your cancerously reproducing starchitect-designed Prada stores, your breathless yak about real estate prices drowning out all civilized conversation, your deafening restaurants impossible to get into, your cheap TV stars muscling out real talent on Broadway, your smelly streets clogged with blacker SUVs with darker-tinted windows ferrying richer and richer hedge-fund creeps. And where does it leave you? Still chasing yesterday's high.

In that moment I loved our new life in dumpy Washington State and especially Joe for dragging me here and saving me from my Manhattan-centric worst self.

"Remember how last year you wouldn't let me get a funnel cake?" was Timby's takeaway. He passed the photo back up.

"Why are you sad?" Timby asked.

"I worry I haven't been paying enough attention to your dad," I said.

"It's okay, Mama. That's just how you are."

I pulled over and rested my forehead on the steering wheel. My breath flittered about high in my chest.

"I don't want to be that way," I said, tears filling my voice. "I really don't."

I unbuckled my seat belt and turned around.

"What are you doing?" Timby asked, his voice edged with alarm.

I was all butt as I attempted to clamber into the back.

"I need to hold you," I grunted, struggling to pull my foot up and over.

"Don't," Timby said, a sitting duck in his car seat. "Mom, stop."

"I want to be worthy of you," I said, panting like childbirth. "You deserve better than me." I became stuck between the console and the roof in an unsightly gargoyle crouch.

"Oh God, look at me," I cried. "I don't know what I'm doing!"

"Neither do I," he said. "Go back."

I screwed my shoulders around to face front. Timby's foot gave me a shove into the driver's seat.

I grabbed my hair at my scalp. "And now on top of everything, I just acted really weird and scary."

"Put it behind you," Timby said. "Good job."

I shifted into drive and headed up Elliott Ave., a busy thoroughfare lined with rail yards, abandoned factories, and crappy teardowns, all on their way to becoming LEED-certified tech hubs. In other words, no pedestrians.

Which is why the one guy hulking north caught my eye.

It couldn't be. I slowed down. It was.

"Oh, come *on*." I rolled down the window and drove abreast of him.

"What?" Timby asked. "Why are you stopping?"

"Alonzo!" I said. "Get in!"

The top half of him kept walking.

"I couldn't do it," he said over the traffic. "I'm not going back."

"I'm in a bus lane," I said. "Get in!"

Alonzo fumingly complied. He was in a royal snit, arms crossed, refusing eye contact. I drove off. The seat-belt alert dinged helpfully, then angrily.

"Seat belt," Timby said.

Alonzo didn't budge.

"Does he have differences?" Timby asked me.

"What differences?" Alonzo said.

"Nothing," I said. "It's just they can't say retarded."

Timby tapped Alonzo on the arm. "Excuse me. May I borrow your phone?"

Alonzo passed it over his shoulder and sat there.

"Alonzo!" I said. "What happened?"

"I walked back in and the first thing I saw was a brick of Christmas bows the size of an ottoman. It sickened me and I reversed direction. Did you know that for years I've been working on a novel? Ben Lerner's agent said I could send it to her when I was done."

"That's terrific!"

"But I can't finish it because my soul is a slaughterhouse."

" 'I have measured out my life with coffee spoons,' " I said in commiseration.

Alonzo pressed his back against the passenger door to get a wider perspective of me. "Thank you. But my hell is a private one."

"Or not," I said. "You know that book deal I have? It's been canceled. My editor doesn't even work in publishing anymore. She's editing cheese in Nyack."

"Oh no!" Timby cried. "Are we poor?"

"You and me?" I continued to Alonzo. "We're artists. We've chosen a path that's ninety-nine percent hardship and rejection. But we're in it together. That's what counts."

"Save it," Alonzo said. "You're a woman with a rich husband. All I have to fall back on is an adjunct professorship. And they're trying to get me fired from that."

"Who is?"

"Color the Core," he pronounced. "Or I should say, some Internet cry-bully from Tacoma with a bullhorn and a Facebook page. Under occupation, it says, conversation starter. Conversation starter! Her worldliness is confined to the echo chamber of social media. She wouldn't know a poem if she wiped her mouth with one."

"What's her beef with you?" I asked.

"She somehow got her hands on my Intro to Poetry syllabus. Too many dead white males for her liking. And now she's *e-distributing* a petition demanding my resignation. Langston Hughes is on my reading list. So is Gwendolyn Brooks. But they're just 'proof of my tokenism.'"

"She can't really get you fired?"

"'The best lack all conviction, while the worst are full of passionate intensity,'" Alonzo said wistfully. "Now college students won't know Yeats said that because he's the root of evil. Along with Walt Whitman and Allen Ginsberg. Oh, and me. You can't forget white ol' me. I'm evil too. I'd offer to die if that would help matters. But nope, she just wants me to lose my house. She's got it all figured out. She's angry, so she must be right."

"I feel like there might be another take on all this," I said. "But diversity happens to be one of the subjects I've proactively chosen not to care about."

"You know what I do when people are arguing?" Timby peeped from the back. "I just agree with the last person."

What's-longer-a-cat-or-a-doughnut? blurted a computerized voice from the backseat.

Startled, I yanked the steering wheel, just missing the curb.

"It's the concussion app," Timby said, holding up the phone. He turned to Alonzo. "Mom hit her head."

"Did she."

"It asks you a question every five minutes," Timby said. "As soon as you can't answer, you need to go to the hospital."

"In most cases a cat," I said. "Happy?"

I'd followed the GPS to a random neighborhood. "Yech, Magnolia. Who would want to live here?"

"In a six-hundred-thousand-dollar house?" Alonzo said. "Me."

"Joe's never mentioned anything about Magnolia," I muttered.

"Forgive me," Alonzo said. "What are we doing?"

"Daddy's been going somewhere without telling Mommy so she got the keys to his car."

Alonzo looked back and forth between Timby and me.

"Since she hit her head, she's been making bad choices," Timby said.

I parked at the spot where the map's dotted line came to an abrupt halt. We were in a development of uniform lots and modern-ish red-brick houses. The whole look was just the other side of groovy, the houses more heavy than light. I was surprised hipsters hadn't discovered it yet. If I got out of today alive, perhaps I would discover it. It might be the perfect place to live out your life and die in your sleep, or at least go trick-or-treating.

I got out of the car.

The neighborhood possessed an eerie tranquility, the front yards with their rhododendrons and one Japanese maple strangely antiseptic.

Why on earth would Joe be coming here? There were no clues to be had.

I looked back. On the dashboard, through the windshield: JAZZ ALLEY. The envelope with our subscription tickets. It had been so light...

I reached in and grabbed the envelope.

"Why do you want that?" Timby asked.

I turned my back and ripped it open.

A single perforated sheet. One ticket for each concert. Joe *had* decided to go it alone.

"Oh no," I said. "Oh-no-no-no."

The door slammed. Alonzo calmly walked to a lawn out of earshot of the car and waited for me on the spongy grass.

"Maybe you want to talk about whatever's going on?" he said.

Muffled music, a heavy beat, a sexed-up singer with an auto-tuned voice: Timby had climbed into the passenger seat and was bouncing happily to "his" music.

I took a breath.

"Somewhere along the way," I said to Alonzo. "My marriage turned into an LLC." I waved the tickets as proof. "Joe and I became two adults joined in the business of raising a child. When we first met, I'd have gone anywhere with the guy. I listened rapturously to whatever he said. I delighted in his every little gesture. You wouldn't believe the places we had sex! We got married, and of course I thought, This is what life is. But it wasn't life. It was youth. And now it's Joe going to jazz by himself and me cracking jokes about how cold and erratic I've become. Twenty years ago I was Johnny Appleseed sowing charm and bon mots. If you stuck your finger in my cheek, it would have sprung back like angel food. Now, my face is a moo shu pancake and people cross the street when they see me coming. And this stomach. It's disgusting."

"For what it's worth," Alonzo said. "I enjoy you."

"You can't possibly."

"Nobody recites poems like you," he said. "You attack them so matter-of-factly, with neither pretense nor portent."

"But I'm an idiot."

"You have beginner's mind," Alonzo said. "But it's a fine mind. You always point out something I hadn't noticed."

"Only," I said, referring to my insight of earlier that day.

"Only," Alonzo seconded.

The muffled pop music became blaring pop music.

Timby had opened the door. "Mom! I figured it out."

Alonzo and I exchanged intrigued looks and walked over.

On the GPS screen under PREVIOUS DESTINATIONS was a list of street names and numbers.

"The address Dad put in was nine hundred."

"Deucedly clever, Mr. Holmes," Alonzo said.

I looked around. We were in front of 915.

Alonzo pointed. Across the street, on the corner, a huge lawn. On the curb, in black-stenciled numbers: *900.*

Beyond the lawn, a low-slung brick building. MAGNOLIA COMMUNITY CENTER. A folding chair propped open a door.

"I don't even know what a community center *is*," I mused.

"Hey, Timby," Alonzo said, leaning into the car. "Can you do a cartwheel?"

"Yeah."

"Good," Alonzo said. "You can teach me."

I gave Alonzo a grateful nod and started across the street.

A voice from the phone in Timby's hand.

What-color-is-celery?

"Celery," I called over my shoulder.

I cut a diagonal across the green expanse toward the open door. On the chair, a jar filled with freshly picked anemones.

From inside, light applause.

I burst in . . .

...to a much smaller room than I'd expected.

In a circle of folding chairs sat ten people with tattoos for twenty. No Joe.

"Welcome," said a bald man in a leather vest. "Are you a newcomer?"

On the walls, posters: EASY DOES IT. KEEP IT SIMPLE. ONE DAY AT A TIME. KEEP COMING BACK.

Uh-oh.

All eyes were on me. Their faces were so compassionate and their spirits so broken, I couldn't help but open up.

"I'm trying to find my husband," I said. "He's six foot two. Brownish hair with gray. Blue eyes. He can't be a drunk. I don't think. But I'm out of ideas. I hit my head. I've got my kid with me. He's outside doing cartwheels with a poet who's essentially my paid friend. I know this is anonymous and all, and you don't like to rat each other out. But I really, really want to find my husband. So maybe if I tell you his name, you don't have to say anything, you can just nod like *All the President's Men*?"

Uncomfortable glances were flying, and how. They finally alighted on the man in the vest.

"If your life is being affected by an addict," he offered gently, "we have literature."

He gestured to a table of pamphlets and books. Beside them, a coffeemaker, a random collection of mugs, and a carton of hazelnut creamer marked SEX ADDICTS ONLY.

"Ohhhh!" I said. "You're sex. My husband isn't *that*."

Perhaps I let some distaste creep into my voice because a woman began to cry softly.

"How about I just go," I said, stepping backward. "Good luck with...the journeys."

I went outside, covered my face with my hands, and stood there groaning.

"You're it!" Timby's voice through the breeze.

I looked up.

Alonzo chased him into a round building at the other end of a breezeway.

In groovy '70s font: PRINCE OF PEACE.

A church. I followed the wide and welcoming path lined with freshly planted flowering kale and purple pansies.

I grabbed a brass door handle the size of a cricket bat and entered a low-ceilinged, carpeted narthex. That's right, narthex. It was on a Word of the Day calendar decades ago and of all the words I'd forgotten, narthex wasn't one.

Alonzo sat at an upright piano against the wall.

"What's your favorite song?" he asked Timby.

"'Love You Hard.'"

"I don't know that one."

"It's by Pansy Kingman," Timby said. "The star of *I Know, Right?*" He noticed me. "Where were you?"

"Nowhere," I said. My eyes ached. Maybe it was from going from sunlight to darkness...I needed to sit down.

"Give me a moment?" I said to Alonzo.

I pulled open the door leading to the main, big church part (*not* a Word of the Day, apparently).

"You're going to church?" Timby asked.

"I'm going into a church."

Alonzo played a perky intro on the piano and began to sing.

"'If it hadn't been for Cotton-Eyed Joe, I'd a been married a long time ago. Where did you come from? Where did you go? Where did you come from, Cotton-Eyed Joe?'"

*

I stepped inside. The church opened up to me. Light filtered in from on high through stained glass. More light through clear side windows. Halogen lights dropped gracefully from long, thin wires. Candles burned in red votives. Incense lingered in the air.

I sat down in a pew and the thoughts flooded.

Bucky quoting Buddha! And I'm the shopping cart with a bum wheel going around in circles. No amount of muscle or determination can break me free. Ivy standing there at the airport, her silence an affirmation that I was the raft and it was time to put me down.

It's obvious why she did it: Bucky's world is built on exclusion. The price of admission is slavish loyalty. After Ivy had exposed the truth about their marriage, it was him or me.

Insight!

Violet once told me, "Change is the goal. Insight is the booby prize." She was right, of course.

I don't want insight. I want my sister back.

I'm sorry, Eleanor, Ivy says to me when she drifts in for her three a.m. hauntings, Joe slumbering peacefully by my side. *It was a sickening choice I had to make. Always know I do see you for who you are. You are my family. I miss you too.*

Then I wake up in a sweat, ditched, a monster gutted of both softness and strength, of every good quality I ever possessed. The next morning I return to my daily life, which is just a mock-up of daily life because of my secret shame: I've been reduced to a thing that misses Ivy.

203

I touched the empty bench at my side, something I find myself doing when I ache for my sister.

The comfort, the thrill to have her sitting beside me. To again have a sister who "always came by," as Spencer had put it. Just imagining Ivy's flesh and her limbs, something within me rose up, the Flood girls one again, ready to conquer the world.

"Excuse me?" It was Timby. He'd cracked the door and poked his head through. "Can you name three countries in Europe?"

"Spain, France, and Luxembourg."

Timby gave me the thumbs-up and closed the door.

I started with a new shrink this week. I told him the tale of the Troubled Troubadour, the one I'd been perfecting all those sleepless nights. In it, Bucky was the villain, I the victim, Ivy the pawn. It was so dispassionate it might have been told by a third party. (The Trick strikes again!) The shrink suggested that the worst thing a person can experience is being on the receiving end of "hatred and misunderstanding."

"What if there were something even worse?" I asked him. "Hatred and *understanding*?"

Everything Bucky had said about me at the airport that day. None of it was wrong.

Would you like to sample a nutty Gouda? Sorry, Joyce Primm, you're selling cheese because you wanted the real story of my life but I'd already drawn an *X* through it.

I raised my face.

The colors of the dusty light were the colors of autumn, the colors of the '70s: orange, mustard, brown, olive. The stained glass looked more inspired by Peter Max or Milton Glaser than Christianity. A hand holding a dove. The word *joy* in sock-it-to-me font. The one depiction of Jesus had him with ropy rainbow hair like the Bob Dylan album cover. Mom came home one Sunday beaming with optimism because the choir had sung "Day by Day" from *Godspell* and the priest had announced that from then on, women would be allowed to wear pants to church. She would be dead within the year.

Daddy used to call the three of us "my girls." Mom called the two of us "my girls." What a dishonor to them both, the shameful estrangement of the Flood girls now.

Building a wall around Ivy, Bucky, and the shambles of the past: it seemed like the only solution at the time. And for years, it had worked. Kinda! But today the wall buckled.

I stood up. My heart was as heavy as an asteroid.

I'd turn fifty in May. My accomplishments? To most people, they'd be the stuff of pipe dreams. Everything I'd set out to achieve in this lifetime, I'd done, with grace to spare. Except loving well the people I loved the most.

It was time to try something else. What, though?

Alonzo and Timby were on their feet, an intense playful energy bouncing between them.

"Where did it go?" Alonzo said. "Wait, there it is!"

"Where?" Timby jumped up and down.

Alonzo reached behind Timby's ear and pulled out a quarter. "There it is! It ain't right!"

Timby grabbed the coin from his hand.

"It ain't right!" Alonzo said, and turned to me. "Any luck?"

"No luck at all," I said.

Together the three of us squinted into the afternoon sun. We headed back down the path toward the car.

The Twelve Step meeting had broken up. Several addicts hung around drinking coffee and smoking. I approached.

"Hi," I said. "I want to apologize again for interrupting."

"Pobody's nerfect," the vested man said.

The fragile woman watched me warily and sipped her coffee. She drank out of a Color Me Mine special. There was no mistaking the mug's thickness and sloppy glaze job.

I thought I was hallucinating.

"Can I see the other side of your mug?" I asked.

She turned it: a childish rendering of a walking stick and the word *Daddy*.

With Timby's backward *Y*.

"Joe," I said. "He was here."

All eyes quickly looked away.

I cried out in frustration. "Is there anyone in the vicinity who is *not* addicted to something? I have one basic question."

"They all left early and took a bus down to the Key," offered a woman leaning over to scratch a cat.

"The Key?" I said.

"The Key Arena."

The Key Arena was part of the Seattle Center, seventy acres in the middle of the city, home of the '62 World's Fair. The pristine campus now boasted five museums, seven theaters, a dozen restaurants, and zero places to park. I bit the bullet and used the valet.

My eye was pulled up the Space Needle towering fantastically overhead, its hot white spotlights beginning to win out over the bruising sky.

"Can I pee?" Timby said.

"Quickly."

"I'll take him," Alonzo offered and they headed into the children's theater.

I went to a deck, leaned against the rail, and looked out across the expanse.

Summer was over: the cheery red popcorn wagon was locked and on its side by a concrete wall. Soft salmon the color on the weeping Japanese maples. Armies arrived each dawn to erase any sign of autumn on the ground; it was only on the trees. The lawn was freshly mowed and striped like vacuumed carpet. Bearded, topknotted men in their twenties walked their bicycles through, tech lanyards swaying. The enormous fountain in the center blasted water up and out, fifty nozzles pointed skyward, all synchronized to music, violent classical, it sounded like from my faraway perch. Kids in various stages of dress dashed up and down the fountain's embankment trying to outrun the unpredictable blasts. Many shivered violently from having failed: it was the eve of winter.

The Key Arena loomed.

Ugly, squat, concrete. It was hard to imagine the thing was ever considered beautiful, even back in '62. The Beatles played there. So did Elvis. It's where the Sonics won the championship. But time had passed it by. The Sonics left for Oklahoma. No NBA team wanted any part of the place. Bands resisted playing there. The logical thing would be to tear it down. But there was always an outcry. Even its defenders couldn't find anything to recommend it other than dogged sentimentality.

Alonzo joined me at the rail.

"I want to go home," I said, feeling a sudden gust of fear. "I don't want to know where Joe's been going."

"I do!" Alonzo said with a laugh.

"Timby, let's go."

But Timby was gone, running down the hill toward a nondescript group of people strolling along, swinging Starbucks.

"Dada!" he cried.

And one of them was Joe.

My mother was represented by the young theatrical agent Sam Cohn before he became the legendary Sam Cohn. She threw him a surprise birthday in our rambling, rent-controlled Upper West Side apartment. Her twist: Each guest had to bring one friend Sam had never met. While all Sam's real friends hid in the back staircase, Sam entered to a roomful of strangers yelling, "Surprise!"

*

Now it was me, scanning the unknown faces, wanting to be relieved to see these people who called up nothing.

They smiled and chatted animatedly as if still trying to make good impressions. The silence of familiarity hadn't yet descended.

Joe spotted Timby. His face lit up. He handed his coffee to one of the strangers just in time for Timby to leap into his arms. Timby's legs were so long it looked like Joe was holding a grown person.

Joe looked around and spotted me at the rail.

I gave him a wave.

Joe shook his head, but not in surprise or remorse. It was almost as if...dare I say...he welcomed the wonder of it all.

The Plan

From where Joe was standing Eleanor was thirty again, in cutoffs and a button-down covered with red roses, her bare feet crusted in sand.

Joe had been two years into his residency then, pulling a graveyard ER shift at Southside Hospital on Long Island. Friday night always delivered revelers with alcohol-related injuries, but never anyone as captivating as the Flood girls.

Ivy was the one your eyes went to, six feet tall, milky skin, ethereal and lissome, her flowing yellow dress blackened at the hem from dragging on the ground. Something about her made you want to reach out and confirm she was real. Eleanor was the hurt one, though, her right arm in a sling made from a bedsheet.

"So tell me what happened," Joe said.

Eleanor had green eyes and a dusting of freckles. Pretty, but not the pretty one.

"You know how you're walking along the beach," she said, and paused to burp. "Excuse me. And you see those share houses with rickety decks and you think, What idiot would be stupid enough to stand on one of those, let alone throw a keg party and pack it with thirty people?"

"The answer is..." Ivy pointed at Eleanor.

"Let's see the damage." Joe rested her arm on a rolling table. He gingerly untied the bedsheet.

Eleanor looked around, as if pillaging the exam room for details. Joe watched her watching. He caught himself and lowered his eyes. They landed on the curve of her waist peeking through a gap between her shirt buttons. He quickly looked away.

Her wrist was badly swollen.

Joe held out his hand. "Can you shake it?"

Eleanor winced, unable to move her fingers.

"I'm right-handed!" she said. "It's how I make a living. If I can't hold a pencil, my life is over."

"Or at least inconvenienced," Ivy put in. To Joe, as if Eleanor weren't in the room: "She tends to exaggerate."

"A life-changing job falls into my lap and what do I do before I even sign the contract?" Eleanor said. "Rent a house on Fire Island and throw a party."

"I wanted it to be a theme party," Ivy said, pouting. "It's midsummer, June twenty-first."

"You dress like Titania every day as it is," Eleanor shot back, then turned to Joe. "What kind of hillbilly move is that? Spending money I don't have on a keg party!"

"Let's get you X-rayed," he said.

"Oh. My. God," Eleanor said. "What's that T-shirt?"

Joe opened his lab coat to check. The one he'd put on in the dark that morning was daffodil yellow with a cheery blue clown and the words *Meyer Mania*.

Ivy came around. Now both sisters had him in their crosshairs.

"Meyer Mania?" said Ivy.

"Yeah," he said, not sharing the excitement. "I've had it forever."

"But what *is* it?" Eleanor asked.

"My theory is a family of Meyers had these T-shirts made for a reunion, and you could get a free image, so they picked a happy clown."

"How did *you* end up with it, though?" Eleanor asked.

"I found it in the dryer at college."

Eleanor grabbed Ivy with her good hand. Ivy grabbed her back.

"What?" Joe asked.

"We may love you," Ivy said.

The X-ray came back showing a significant Colles' fracture. Joe returned to the examination room to find the sisters yammering about the party.

"I'm surprised you're not in more pain," he told Eleanor.

"Oh, I'm in pain," Eleanor said. "Pain I'm good with. It's discomfort I can't handle."

"You win!" Ivy said, poking Eleanor.

Eleanor yipped; for a moment the laughing sisters were lost in each other.

Ivy explained it to Joe. "We have a contest. We each try to prove we have a weaker character than the other."

Joe tried to do the math on that.

"You get twenty bonus points," Eleanor said to Ivy. "My life is over and you're staring at yourself."

Ivy was on tiptoes, looking over her shoulder at her reflection in a clerestory.

"Someone give Narcissus a hand mirror before she climbs onto the counter," Eleanor said.

"Her career isn't over, right?" Ivy asked.

"Nah," Joe said. "I'll put her in a short cast and she'll be holding a pencil in two weeks."

"A cast?" Eleanor cried. " 'Hello, Violet Parry? I was on a deck that collapsed and I broke my wrist so you'll have to find another animation director.'" Her voice jumped an octave. "Why now? Why my right hand? Things were finally starting to go well—"

"Stop talking," Joe said, surprised at the forcefulness of his tone. More surprising, Eleanor did stop talking.

"Oh, my," Ivy whispered.

"The world isn't your friend," Joe told Eleanor. "It's not designed to go your way. All you can do is make the decision to muscle through and fight the trend."

Eleanor's face spread into a smile. "And call you on Monday."

"And call me on Monday."

"Oh, my." This time, Ivy said it out loud.

Twenty years and Timby later, apartments bought and sold, belongings packed and unpacked, a move across the country, funerals of parents, career triumphs and washouts: how could Joe tell Eleanor his path had been leading somewhere that didn't involve her?

That for fifty years there'd been a hidden architecture to his life, like the aisle lights in the floor of an airplane. They're always there, embedded in the ordinariness of the plane; no need to notice them until there's an emergency and they blink on to lead you to safety.

It came with no warning. A month ago. On a breezy Sunday, the day of the Seahawks home opener. As usual, Joe had arrived at the Clink two hours early to take care of the players.

First up, Vonte Daggatt, a star safety who'd sustained a severe distal radius fracture at the end of last season. Joe had operated immediately, inserting a titanium plate. The bone had healed nicely over the summer. There'd been minor swelling on Wednesday; Joe hoped the cortisone shot would have eased it enough to clear Vonte to play.

Coach Carroll, chewing his three sticks of gum, paced outside the exam room. In five minutes he had to submit his final roster; he needed Vonte on it.

"How does this feel?" Joe squeezed Vonte's wrist, watching for a wince.

"Pretty good," Vonte said with a loaded smile. He knew Joe knew he'd say anything to get out there and play.

"Any stiffness?" Joe asked.

"You know."

Gordy, a trainer, stood at attention. Joe turned to him.

"Let's do a padded splint."

"Thanks, Doc," Vonte said.

Pete Carroll stepped in. "We good, then?"

Joe gave the nod.

"Ready to play some ball?" Pete gave Vonte a big, sloppy shake.

"All in God's plan," Vonte said.

"You mean all in the Sanders Splint Supply's plan," Joe said.

"My plan now." The coach headed out, full of vim. "Thanks, Joe!"

"Got the whole family here," Vonte said as Joe cut the foam.

"My wife too," Joe said. "Her first game."

"First game?" Vonte's head jerked back. He launched into a long, sympathetic laugh. "Man, oh, man."

Joe said nothing.

Eleanor not going to games had been understandable at first; over time, it grew annoying; over more time, it felt like a personal dig. Which was why Joe had insisted she come today.

Joe applied the splint himself. It would give Vonte's wrist good stability but allow full movement of the fingers.

"First pick-six is for you, Doc," Vonte said.

"I'd expect nothing less," said Joe.

Joe followed up with other players and their minor dings. A sore knee. A back spasm. A sprained toe from a barbecue flip-flop accident.

Close to game time, Joe found himself in the flow of players and personnel making their way to the field. Spirits were high but not too high. It boded well for a win.

The team waited for their cue in the shadowy mouth of the tunnel. Out on the field, men rolled fire-shooting columns into place. The Sea Gals formed their glamorous gauntlet. Yellow-vested video crews swarmed. When the camera lights hit, the players pressed together in an amoeba-like cluster, bouncing and chanting.

Joe ducked out of the way and found his friend Kevin, another team physician who'd agreed to run lead today on account of Eleanor's rare appearance.

"I'll be in the stands," Joe told him.

"Cool," Kevin said. "I'll text if we need you."

Joe pulled out his shiny ticket and headed up.

He emerged from the pleasantly echoing concrete of the concourse into a swaying, sparkling ocean, the seventy thousand fans an undulation of blue. White lights set the field ablaze in freakishly fake green. The September sky felt moody with patches of black; wisps of clouds rushed overhead. A twist of wind brushed Joe's face. He breathed in the salty air.

This.

Jeopardy! champ and Seattle native Ken Jennings hoisted the 12 flag, then rushed to the rail, whipping a rally towel over his head, twirling the ecstatic crowd into a frenzy. Even the kickoff siren couldn't compete with the ear-busting roar. The stadium quaked underfoot.

Kickoff!

The Cardinal return man signaled fair catch. The fans registered their disappointment, ripples on the sea.

Joe lingered on the promenade, basking in the optimism. How he wished Timby were here! First thing Monday, Joe would submit a ticket request for every home game. On his way out, he'd hit the fan shop and scoop up matching jerseys.

"We'll take that if you're not using it." A pair of shopworn blondes with blue-and-green streaked hair made puppy eyes at Joe and the ID around his neck: FIELD AND LOCKER ROOM ACCESS.

Joe chuckled and tucked the lanyard inside his shirt. He started down the popcorn-littered stairs. Every few steps a tipsy white dude high-fived him.

"Seahawks!" screamed one who'd forgotten he was holding a beer. A wave of amber grain sloshed onto his fingers. He slurped at them lovingly.

Every face said what didn't need to be spoken: *We made it inside this place, the best place.* The collective pride buoyed Joe as he made his way to row J.

His seat was six in. He scanned the row for Eleanor. Perhaps she hadn't arrived yet.

"Sorry, folks," Joe said cheerily, making his way to his seat. "Hate to do this."

Eleanor *was* there. Sitting, legs crossed, hugging the purse in her lap. She stood to let Joe pass.

"Hey, babe!" Joe had to yell. "Can you believe this craziness?"

"I know! The rows are like sliced prosciutto. You have to be Flat Stanley to get by."

"That too," he said, and gave her a peck on the cheek.

"Oh!" she said. "I just stopped by the hospitality suite. Have you been?"

"I don't think so."

The Cardinal offense had taken the field. The first play of the year, a running play. Gain of five.

"Gah," Joe said. "We should have stopped that."

Those around him grumbled in stressed-out agreement.

"All they have there," Eleanor was saying, "is bottles of room-temperature water, SunChips, and a giant bowl of watery fruit salad. It looked canned. At least the apples were fresh. You know how I know?"

"Honey," Joe said. "The game."

A pass play, the Cardinals quarterback going long...broken up...by Vonte!

"There's my man!" Joe cheered.

A riot of high-fives, Joe giving and getting the love from all sides.

Two rows down, four jerseys bobbed: DAGGATT, DAGGATT, DAGGATT, DAGGATT. Vonte's family. Joe recognized them from the hospital. His wife, Chrissy, going bananas as the girls, Michaela, Asia, and Vanessa, took videos of the video replay.

Joe sensed something near his face.

Eleanor's thumb. On it, the sticker from an apple.

"Look what I almost choked on!" she said, grinning.

A sudden rush of dark thoughts grabbed Joe by the throat.

She doesn't want to be here. She doesn't like anything I like. Jazz, documentaries, bike rides. If it's not her idea, she'll sit there making disturbing grimace-y faces. My wife is a solo act. She's always been a solo act. Why am I just seeing it now?

"You don't have to stay," he said.

"Huh?"

"The plan wasn't to torture you," he said. "The plan was for us to enjoy the game together."

Eleanor's whole being settled; her face relaxed. "Have I told you lately that I love you?"

Joe chuckled. It was their least favorite Van Morrison song.

"I can't hear you!" a voice boomed. Macklemore, pretaped, hamming it up on the Diamond Vision.

Third down. Every fan knew what to do: Stand up and scream their guts out. Joe joined in, shrieking through cupped hands.

He turned to Eleanor. She wasn't there.

Over his shoulder, between the fans, he saw her zipping up the stairs, two at a time.

Unbelievable.

She'd actually fucking left.

Her seat was still down. The disbelief, the outrage, the alienation.

The empty chair.

Joe stumbled backward, one foot landing squarely on a clear plastic Seahawks tote. He picked it up. It was full of cracked makeup.

Clap. Clap. Clap.

Three frat bros standing above did the slow, sarcastic clap.

Green sparkly fingernails snatched the bag. A pissed-off woman in a pink camouflage T-shirt with a sequined *12* whimpered in dismay.

"I'm sorry," Joe said.

"Walk much?" her husband quipped.

"My favorite rouge!" the woman cried. "Now the hinges are cracked."

Clap. Clap. Clap.

Something within Joe awakened. His eyes darted between the frat guys and the husband and wife.

"For real?" he said.

To a person, they averted their gazes.

Joe got the hell out.

Shaky, he jogged along the promenade, back through the section tunnel, and along the concession stands with their meaty, yeasty, cloying smell-storms. He pushed down the stairs past agitated latecomers. Up on a platform, a shiny Toyota truck frozen in mid-adventure, tilted, about to flip.

He flashed his pass at the guard posted outside the blue curtain. The restricted area. He followed the blue-and-green stripe on the concrete floor. It veered left.

Overhead: FIELD ACCESS THROUGH THESE DOORS.

"Dr. Wallace!" Another guard, Mindy, a secret Colts fan, stepped aside to let Joe through.

In giant blue letters along the white cinder-block hallway:

GET THE WIN.

ALWAYS COMPETE.

LET'S DO THIS.

NEVER QUIT.

Joe's stomach seized from the harsh smack of the words.

Another rush of dark thoughts.

The sending money to my parents. The charity trips. The fund-raising. The twenty-six-hour flights to Kenya. The extra time I take with patients. The lifting weights at the WAC. The cute links I send Eleanor. The steam engine built with Timby. The showers before getting into the pool. Notes praising helpful customer-service people.

Picking up garbage off the sidewalk. Trips to the e-waste center. Keeping the thermostat at sixty-eight. Not wasting dinner rolls. Letting other cars into traffic. Mnemonics to remember the names of the OR staff. Salt-free potato chips. Games of Clue. Colonoscopies. Giving Eleanor the better parking space. The weekly hardcover purchase at Elliott Bay. Resoling shoes. Tipping hotel maids. Refilling growlers. Punctuating text messages—

Boom! The thud of a cannon going off on the field.

Coming toward him down the tunnel: A bird of prey. Eye level. The real, live Seattle sea hawk, perched on its handler's gloved arm. Joe locked eyes with the bird as he passed. The raptor held Joe's stare, head gliding around, its penetrating gaze suggesting both wisdom and weariness.

Joe's shoulders jerked with tension. He stepped out onto the turf.

The Sea Gals jogged up in formation and took their places, eight across, two deep, and began a lurid shimmy to "Dirty Deeds Done Dirt Cheap." Makeup thick as tree bark, man-made cleavage, flesh-colored tights: a living affront to the natural world.

Joe looked away.

The Cardinals had the ball again; the 'Hawks must have gone three and out. The coaches and players were clustered at the far end of the field.

Joe spotted Gordy at the fifty. Just the sight of the trainer brought Joe a tickle of relief: his people.

Gordy was joking with the team "flexibility specialist," basically a yoga teacher, a little guy with spindly legs who always wore a bandanna. He said something that had Gordy cracking up.

Joe picked up his pace, eager to join the camaraderie.

But then, in Gordy's hand: a splint. *The* splint.

Joe scanned the action. Their defense was getting into position. He found number 27.

His back to Joe. DAGGATT.

Joe's whole body juddered in disbelief. He stormed toward the trainer.

"What the fuck, Gordy?"

Gordy turned. He knew how bad this was.

The yoga teacher got out of the line of fire.

"Vonte wanted to try a possession without it," Gordy said, panic cracking his voice. "He was feeling good."

"Not your call."

"We're cool," said the yoga teacher.

"No," Joe snapped. "We're not cool."

"He almost made the pick—" Gordy stammered.

"What, you have him on your fantasy team or something? You have one concern: to make sure none of those men have a career-ending injury."

"I know." Gordy looked on the verge of vomiting.

"That's his livelihood! These guys have ten years in them if they're lucky! He has three daughters!"

"I know."

"You don't fucking know!" Joe got in his face. "Stop saying you know!"

The yoga teacher got between them.

"Hey, bro, relax."

"You don't talk to me!" Joe bellowed.

"Let's dial this whole thing down," the yoga teacher cooed. His orange bandanna was covered in a logo—

GODADDY.

Joe shoved the yoga teacher, hard.

"The hell?" Gordy cried —

The yoga teacher flew back and almost went down —

But was saved by his remarkable balance —

And sprang back up.

Joe charged again, this time slamming the bewildered yogi to the turf. Joe drew back his fist and —

From behind, a big pair of arms clamped him in a bouncer hold.

"That's enough!" Kevin, his friend, hustled Joe off the field.

"They let Daggatt go out without his splint!" Joe raged.

"Joe, man, pull it together!" Kevin shouted over the cacophonous 70,000.

Joe looked back.

A consternated ref was trotting over to Gordy and the dazed yoga teacher, who was now standing, one foot inbounds.

Kevin stepped into Joe's line of sight. "I'll deal with it. Just go inside. Go!" Kevin gave Joe a hefty push toward the tunnel.

"C'mon, man!" Voices. "C'mon, man!" Heckling voices. Hanging off the rail overhead and on both sides: potbellied, faces painted, green-Afroed, tongues out, drunk before noon. "C'mon, man!" Jeering at Joe.

He reeled into the tunnel. Vertigo hit. The fact of what he had just done. It raised his head off his shoulders and made it wobble, left and right, around and around. He teetered against the cold cinder-block wall.

"Need something, Doc?" Yet another guard, sitting and watching the game on a phone balanced on his big knee.

A door. The press room. Empty now. Joe lunged for the knob.

Pete Carroll's lectern. Seahawks wallpaper. Rows of empty chairs. More chairs stacked, so high they seemed to sway. Joe closed the door behind him.

A tomblike quiet descended.

Joe, jangly, panting, his heartbeat on the fritz.

He took it.

He took it.

Until he couldn't take it.

He slumped onto a bench and pressed the heels of his hands into his eye sockets.

Med school, dedication, integrity, restraint: all a cosmic sideshow. All a laughable, flimsy work-around. Over now. Undone in an instant.

Joe moved his palms to his forehead and opened his eyes. He stared at the carpet tile.

"It can't be as bad as all that," said a voice with a British accent.

The crinkling of newsprint.

Joe wasn't alone.

Sitting on a chair in the corner, legs crossed, reading the Travel section: a man Joe had never seen. Fifties with short gray hair and little round glasses. No ID badge. Hiking boots and a vest over a long white shirt.

"Perhaps I can be of help."

And now, Eleanor across the lawn, the Space Needle at her back. They'd gone through so much together. They were about to go through more.

Now's the time, God was saying.

Tell her.

The Art of Losing

The fact that Joe did *not* look caught or panicked or any of the normal emotions a husband might feel when totally busted: my immediate reaction was fury.

I pushed myself off the rail and flounced through the café tables of people eating foodcourt. When I hit the path at the top of the hill, the pitch swept me into a jog. But with every step, I felt my anger falling away. Underneath that anger: fear.

In the middle of one of her self-help phases, Ivy had once proclaimed that underneath all anger was fear. I'd long since wondered what, if anything, was underneath all fear.

I knew then: If underneath anger was fear, then underneath fear was love. Everything came down to the terror of losing what you love.

I ran to Joe and pulled him in. I pushed my face into his jacket and breathed in the wool and dry-cleaning. Joe's height was always a narcotic for me, the way my head hit him at the chest. I dug my fingers under his shoulder blades and turned my cheek so my nose touched flesh. The dampness of his clavicle, the tickle of his chest hair. The smell of Joe. My man.

"Hey!" he said. "Hello to you too."

Alonzo arrived and introduced himself.

"A face to the name." Joe shook Alonzo's hand. A fluorescent wristband peeked from under Joe's cuff.

"Mommy and I have been looking for you all day," Timby said.

"We went to your office and they thought you were on vacation and then Mom drove your car on that superlong bridge that goes up a hill."

"Oh." Joe's eyes met mine and instantly dropped to the asphalt.

"It doesn't matter," I said.

Joe tightened his lips and looked at me. A deep breath.

"I don't want to know—" I started.

"I found religion."

"Religion?" I said. This was too weird. "Religion?"

"Hunh," Alonzo said.

"What do you mean, religion?" I asked. "Religion in kettle bells? Religion in Radiohead?"

"Religion in Jesus."

"Can I get a snack?" Timby said, no dummy.

"I'll go too," Alonzo said, and hustled Timby off.

It was Joe. My husband.

"It was the last thing I expected too," he said, shifting uncomfortably. "But I flipped out at work."

"Okay…"

"I came across a man," Joe said. "An ordinary man. A pastor. He invited me to his church."

"And you *went?*" I said.

"I know," he said. "And that's where it happened."

"What happened?"

"We were just people," Joe said, "coming together. The collective humility overwhelmed me. Simon, the pastor, began his sermon. It was about Christ entering the Temple, the money changers, a story I'd heard a million times. But Simon put it in historical perspective. And it felt so relevant and even radical."

"Relevant to *you?*"

"It spoke of the courage and wisdom of Jesus the man. I felt a thousand-pound weight being lifted off my shoulders and gently placed on the ground. The lifting was done by a human presence. I looked around and everything had changed. Nothing separated me from the people, the light, the smells, the trees. I was bathed—we were all bathed—in a radiant love."

"So you had a bad day," I said.

"I had a direct experience of God."

"Therefore you lied to me?" A bitter brew of betrayal and self-pity gurgled within. "When were you going to share this wonderful news?"

"I know," Joe said, rubbing my arm.

I jerked away. "Just because you're calmer than I am doesn't mean you're morally superior."

A family on a Segway tour of Seattle zoomed by, all smiles.

"What do you think when you hear *God's plan?*" Joe asked.

"I think you've been talking to too many Seahawks."

"I want you to consider the possibility that we live in a benevolent universe."

"Consider it considered."

"*Really* consider it," Joe said. "If the universe is benevolent, that means everything is going to turn out okay. It means we can stop trying to punch our way out of the gunnysack."

"Will you please admit that everything you're saying is profoundly weird?"

"It couldn't be more sensible," Joe said. "Instead of trying to impose your will on an uncontrollable universe, you can surrender to the wisdom of Jesus."

"Please stop saying Jesus. People might think we're poor."

"I'm acutely aware that becoming a Christian is the least cool thing a person can do." He looked at his phone. "Oh! They need me. We have sound check."

"Sound check?"

"We're singing for the Pope on Saturday."

"You're what?" I said dully.

"Singing for the Pope at Key Arena. A multidenominational celebration. My congregation is taking part."

I had to grab a tree for support. "You're seriously putting together the words 'my' and 'congregation?'"

He gave me a hug. "I'm so glad it happened this way. You showing up like you did. See how it all works out when you let it?"

"Is that what you call this?" I said, squirming to escape his mawkish embrace. *"Working out?"*

"We'll talk about everything when I get home." He stuck his hands in the pockets of his sport coat and disappeared down the steps to the Key Arena.

Leaving me standing there, whacked.

"You need a wristband," the Key Arena guard said. He stood beside a metal detector and folding table. Beyond him, glass doors with more guards.

"My husband has a wristband," I said, my whole body hopping. "He just went in." I was in a panic to get inside, to get Joe off this insanity.

"Nope," the guy said.

At his side, a German shepherd. Embroidered on its harness, PLEASE DO NOT PET ME.

A group of schoolchildren in matching T-shirts bounded up carrying giant Slurpees, their weary teachers at the rear.

"You're blocking the entrance," the guard said to me over the racket. To the kids rushing toward the dog, "Read the harness."

"Just please?" I said, getting jostled by sugar-pumped munchkins. "My husband's a doctor. I hit my head." I lifted my bangs and revealed my bump. "See? I'm capable of anything."

"Except going inside."

"Do I look like a woman who wants to blow up the Pope?"

He shot me a hard look. "That's not something we joke about, ma'am." He grabbed his clipboard and turned to a teacher.

As he did, a sheet of neon-green wristbands fell to the ground. I bent down, pretending to tie my shoe, and tore one off. I palmed it and sprang back up.

I hurried to the next entrance, flashed my wrist, and sailed through.

Dim fluorescent lights gave off a sickly glow. Crew members hoisted colorful banners up into the rafters. On the third tier, cops led bomb-sniffing German shepherds from seat to seat.

"One-two, one-two," blatted a voice over the sound system.

On the stage, union guys set up a forest of oversize foam-core happy people, ball-headed, arms raised in joyous *V*s.

On the floor, in folding chairs, groups of singers waited to rehearse. Tibetan monks, an African American choir, Sikhs in turbans, and, loosely assembled in three or four rows at the front, Joe's group. I shot down the steps and slid in behind him.

"Here's the thing," I said.

Joe turned. "What are you doing?"

"We all want to give up," I said. "You don't need Jesus for that. Look at me. I've given up all on my own."

"Is this Eleanor?" said an Englishman one row up. He had on a white tunic and a khaki vest.

Joe introduced Simon, the Seahawks chaplain.

"You're the one who brainwashed my husband?"

"It would seem!" he said, shaking my hand.

"Simon leads the team in prayer before and after the games," Joe said. "In between, he hangs out in the press room."

"It's a good time to catch up on my *New Yorker*s," Simon offered. "I have stacks." He held one up, then turned back around.

"So you're on some kind of church kick?" I asked Joe.

"It's bigger than that," he said. "It's radical transformation."

Those are words no wife wants to hear.

"Radical which includes me," I stated or asked or pleaded. Whatever it was, my voice broke and my mouth filled with tears.

"Of course it does," Joe said, taking my hand. "We can talk about it when I get home." He looked pointedly at those within earshot and nodded at me, as if the whole conversation were over.

"But you were happy," I said. "You *are* happy."

"Eleanor, I attacked a yoga teacher."

"I'm sure he deserved it," I said.

"For wearing a GoDaddy bandanna."

"Twenty years," I said, "you've been telling me religion is for reality-dodgers. That no one with an education and an IQ could possibly believe in God."

"Do you hear your arrogance?" Joe asked.

"It's *your* arrogance!" I said. "You're the big atheist."

"Call it a loss of faith," he said. "I lost my faith in atheism."

"I like that," Simon mused. "A lot." He patted his pockets for a pen.

"Atheism, skepticism, always having to be right," Joe continued. "It was my way of staying comfortably numb." He pointed to Simon and proudly added, "I'm sure he knows the reference."

" 'My hands felt just like two balloons'!" Simon said.

Commotion broke out on the stage. Crewmen shouted to clear the way for a forklift grinding up the ramp. It deposited a six-foot crate and spun around cutely before making its exit. Electric drills whined as the crate was unscrewed.

"What does radical transformation even mean?" I asked Joe.

"He'll tell you at home," bleated a woman, heavyset and with a flat affect. She could have worked at the DMV.

Joe smiled and raised his eyebrows, as if that settled it.

"No," I said. "Now."

Everyone was looking at us. Black and white, old and young. To a person they needed moisturizer.

"Okay," Joe said. "I'm thinking of going to divinity school."

"Boom," said the DMV lady with a chuckle.

"Nothing has captivated me like Jesus Christ," Joe said.

"You have no idea how hard this is for me." I closed my eyes and pinched the bridge of my nose. "It's like you've just gone from the most interesting person I've ever met to the least interesting person I've ever met."

"Jesus was the most radical thinker in world history," Joe said. "I want to learn everything about first-century Palestine. About the Temple culture of Jerusalem. I want to study the Gnostic gospels, the Nag Hammadi texts."

"Aren't there podcasts?"

"I want to be taught," Joe said. "I've been working like a fiend on my applications—"

"Hang on," I said. "Is that where you've been the past week?"

"At Starbucks, writing my essays."

"Which Starbucks?"

"Does it matter?" he said. "The one on Melrose and Pine."

"That's a good Starbucks." One mystery solved. "What were you looking at with that spy thing on your desk?"

"The spotting scope," Joe said. "I was looking at the stars."

"The stars?" I said. "What stars? Oh, don't tell me. God's stars."

He didn't argue. I sighed. All I could do was marvel at how wrong I'd been.

Up onstage, the crate had been opened. In it, an object covered in bubble wrap. As a woman carefully cut away the multiple layers, a chair was revealed. A throne, in fact, with a crimson seat and high back.

"There's a whole lot of Pope going on," I said to Joe. "Does this mean you're Catholic again?"

"No, no, no," he said. "You can't be Catholic. But it *is* the Pope. You gotta show up."

Center stage, a union guy with a Ramones T-shirt sat on the Pope's throne as the spotlight got adjusted.

"But Jesus?" I asked. "Why can't it be something normal, like Buddhism? I already have the cushion."

He shook his head. "It's Jesus. Jesus is my guy."

The union worker on the throne loudly proclaimed into the mic, "The great Oz has spoken!"

Titters from the crew.

"Rick!" came a voice from the sound system. "Not cool."

Joe took my hand. "You know how we agreed to live ten years in Seattle for me, then ten years in New York for you?"

"Actually, I do."

"Ten years is up. That's why I applied to Columbia."

"*Columbia?* So on top of everything else, I'm supposed to pack up and leave all my friends?"

"You don't like your friends," Joe said.

"That's a different conversation."

"If you prefer," he said, "there's a school in Spokane."

"Now you've got me preferring *Spokane?*"

"There's Duke," he said, maintaining his inside voice. "University of Chicago. St. Andrews in Scotland."

"Did you just say Scotland?" I sprang to my feet. "You don't just decide we're moving to Scotland without consulting me! Timby's in school. When were you going to tell me?"

"Tonight!" a knitting woman cried.

"How do you work for the Seahawks from Scotland?"

"We're going to have to make some decisions."

"You got that right."

Now Joe was on his feet. Any pretense that we weren't the kind of couple who fought in public, well, that veil had just fallen.

"What I'm going through is new and fragile," Joe said.

"Which is why you let it pass! You don't become a Jesus freak! Where's the goddamned pride?"

"I knew how hard this would be for you," Joe shot back.

"So of course you just lied!"

"I'm not a liar!" he said. "I hated lying." His voice went soft. "But I felt trapped."

That hit me…hard.

"Eleanor?" Joe said.

"That's why you were facedown at the breakfast table," I said, reeling. "It was because of me. This whole thing is my fault."

"*Fault?*"

Beside us was a forest of six-foot-high potted palms, stage dressing waiting to be set. I went over and slid a bunch of pots aside with my foot, creating a path. I took Joe by the hand and led him inside the oasis. It was just us.

I placed my hands on his shoulders. "I know what this is."

"You do?"

"I'm the one who should have your back. Not Jesus."

"Eleanor," Joe said gently. "God's bigger than you. That's kind of the whole point."

"You couldn't lean on me," I said. "I was too rickety. I was too all over the place. And I know why. I'm still messed up about Bucky and Ivy."

"Them?" he said, swatting palm fronds from his face.

"I thought I could shove them into quarantine. But it doesn't work. Do you want to know how fragmented my brain is? Last week, on the radio, it said a train in Ohio derailed because someone had left a backhoe on the tracks. And I actually thought, Was it me? Did *I* leave a backhoe on the tracks?"

"You're distracted," Joe said. "I'll give you that."

"So distracted that I've driven you into the River Jordan!"

"This is *my* path," Joe said. "*My* struggle."

"I know you think that," I said. "But listen to me. Since we fell in love, I've been keeping a Gratitude List."

"Have you been following the Hubble telescope?" he said.

"Heh?"

"They recently aimed it at the most boring and empty patch of sky they could find. After collecting light for weeks, it found ten thousand galaxies *thirteen billion* light-years away. The human mind can't comprehend that. And it goes the other way too. The smallest particle used to be a grain of sand. Then a molecule, then an atom, then an electron, then a quark. Now it's a string. You know what a string is? It's a *millionth of a billionth of a billionth of a billionth of a centimeter.* But *I* was going around like *I* had it all figured out? And where did it lead me? To wig out at a Seahawks game! That's over now. I'm welcoming the mystery. I'm comforted by the mystery."

"Okay, okay," I said. "I feel like we're getting away from the Gratitude List."

"Prince of Peace!" a voice called over the loudspeaker.

Through the dense green crosshatch, Joe's group rose, leaving behind their purses and jackets. Twenty folks, none looking great from behind, trudged up the stairs.

"If you go up there," I said, frustration quickening to panic, "you're giving up on our marriage."

"Eleanor..." Joe said.

"I've been neglecting you," I said, beginning to crumble. "I didn't mean to. But we can't turn into one of those couples who live on parallel tracks. Oh, Eleanor, she locks herself in her closet and draws her pictures and even her own son says, 'Mom, that's just how you are,' but don't you worry about Joe, Joe's got his church friends." Tears, snot, drool, it was all happening.

A stage manager had arranged the choir on risers. People were muttering, looking for Joe.

"Our marriage and me finding God?" Joe said. "They're not connected."

"Prince of Peace!" a voice said from the stage. "We need one more."

"What if I convince you they are?" I said to Joe.

He thought about it for a moment, which made his answer all the more devastating. "It would make no difference."

In an exit worthy of Christ himself, Joe stepped through the plant wall and vanished.

I was alone, pulsing with sorrow and bewilderment.

Humor hadn't worked. Smarts hadn't worked. Brinkmanship, nastiness, insight, self-criticism, desperation, threats: none had worked. The Trick had failed.

The Trick had never failed.

I took a seat.

The stage manager placed Joe in the back row, one in from the right.

I had an almost physical reaction that Joe hadn't been given a spot of greater prominence. Granted, I didn't know who these other people were. But he was Joe Wallace.

My husband. As soon as he wakes up, he jumps right out of bed, showers, and gets fully dressed. Tucks in his shirt, puts on a belt. He never steps out of a cab until the driver has finished telling his story. We still sleep in a queen-size bed because our first night in a new king he said he felt too far away, and we sent it back. He does the Friday and Saturday crosswords in pen. He's my answer man. How many cups in a quart? How long would it take to drive to Yellowstone? What's Zaire called now, or is it called Zaire now but used to be something else? Even better? He puts up with my crap without seeing it as crap.

A young couple stood to the side. The man strummed a guitar; his wife conducted the chorus.

Morning has broken like, the first morning,
Blackbird has spoken like the first bird.

Joe's face grew serious as he began to sing. Joe the choir boy, returned to the flock...

Praise for the singing, praise for the morning,
Praise for them springing fresh from the Word.

A spotlight hit the group. Someone from the rafters adjusted it.

That still August day on Violet and David's lawn. The fawn sand, the bottle-green ocean. Joe in a navy suit with a grape-purple tie and a snowy gardenia in his lapel. The vow I took, looking into Joe's eyes with Ivy at my side, was to help him become a better version of himself.

This *was* the best version of Joe. I saw it with my own eyes. I'd always assumed his becoming that better person would involve me.

Sweet the rain's new fall, sunlit from heaven,
Like the first dewfall on the first grass.

Perhaps it was the pool of light. Perhaps it was Joe's closed eyes. Perhaps it was his blossoming smile. Perhaps it was that Joe was literally on a higher plane than I was. But a river of light seemed to flow over his head; it was made of love, and Joe could dive in anytime he chose, with or without me.

Praise for the sweetness, of the wet garden,
Sprung in completeness where His feet pass.

My eyes pooled with tears. My lungs were butterfly wings. A seed had been sown in the pit of my belly. It grew speedily, blackly, like a Fourth of July snake pellet, a grotesque crinkly thing, filling me up something terrible. I had to look away.

On the empty chair beside me, sticking out of my purse, was my folded-up "Skunk Hour."

a mother skunk with her column of kittens
swills the garbage pail.
She jabs her wedge-head in a cup

of sour cream, drops her ostrich tail,
and will not scare.

I looked up. The choir had shifted, so Joe was blotted out by these others.

Mine is the sunlight, mine is the morning,
Born of the one light Eden saw play.

The African American woman with the purple blouse? She too could have lost her mother to lung cancer when she was nine. The man with the Michael Landon hair? His sister might have mystifyingly turned against him too. Simon? His father could have been a drunk, abandoning him and his brother to fend for themselves, neither knowing when he'd be back, if he'd be back.

And Joe? We had a child together.

Praise with elation, praise every morning,
God's re-creation of the new day.

Joe, who will not scare.

"How dare you!" I shrieked, hurtling over chairs, knocking over coffees, sending purses tumbling to the floor.

"This isn't a fair fight!" I said. "Leave me for another woman, don't leave me for Christ!"

I tripped on the stage steps and crawled the rest of the way. The choir, the stage crew, the guy hanging in the air on a rope ladder, the man holding a foam-core happy person: they all froze.

"Where's the man I bought?" I said, rising to my feet. "I bought a surgeon who thinks for himself and knows things! I bought Joe the Lion. I didn't buy some comfort-seeking sissy boy!"

As I charged Joe, I heard the squawk of a walkie-talkie.

I turned. My friend the security guard.

The words: PLEASE DO NOT PET ME.

Before the dog clamped down on my forearm, I remember thinking, That's something you rarely see...a German shepherd flying through the air.

I opened my eyes.

I was in one of Joe's examination rooms in a padded reclining chair. Beside me was a blue paper screen through which my left arm poked. Joe did this for patients he didn't put under general so they wouldn't look down and reflexively move their hands during surgery.

I was groggy. From a painkiller?

I felt a tightness to my face. With my free hand I started opening drawers until I found a hand mirror. A neat line of stitches under my jaw stopped at my chin. There wouldn't be a scar. Joe was the best closer in the business.

"Are you awake?" It was Timby, sitting in the corner, drawing in a spiral notebook.

"Hi, sweetie." I winced. My jaw was wood, splintering with each small movement.

"Daddy said after the dog bit your arm you fell off the stage!"

A voice from the hallway. "Let me pop in to say good-bye."

Alonzo appeared, followed by a classically pretty blonde wearing pastel-pink cashmere and a black purse with a gold chain strap. Alonzo introduced his wife, Hailey.

"Thank you for today," Alonzo said to me.

All we could do was look into each other's eyes and smile. We just liked each other; we always had. At our first poetry lesson, we'd cried over Robert Frost's "After Apple-Picking"; the waitress had asked, "Did you two just get engaged?"

How-is-a-corkscrew-like-a-hammer?

Alonzo reached into his pocket. "Time to delete this app."

"Aww-uhh!" said a disappointed Timby.

"They're both tools," Hailey said. "And they both have handles." She cutely blew the smoke off a finger pistol and returned it to an imaginary holster.

"This morning," I said to Alonzo. "I'm sorry for calling you 'my poet.'"

"That was okay," he said. "Although I wasn't thrilled to be stuck with the breakfast bill. And the gift-basket bill. And you didn't pay me my fifty bucks."

"Plus he bought me fudge at the Center House," Timby added.

I gasped, mortified. "Is my wallet around?"

"Let's roll it forward," Alonzo said.

Joe was in the doorway now. "Hey, babe." He turned to Alonzo and Hailey. "I'll let you out. It's tricky after hours."

"Until next week," Alonzo said.

"'At the Fishhouses,'" I said.

"Let's do a different Elizabeth Bishop," he said. "'One Art,' it's called."

"'One Art.' I somehow sense it's an indictment of me."

"Quite the opposite," he said.

"Hailey?" I said. "I love this guy."

"Everyone does." She beamed, and they headed out.

It was just me and Timby.

"Look, Mom. I drew you."

by: Timby Wallace

Age: 8

Mommy

"Oh, baby," I said. "I don't want to be Mad Mommy."

"So don't."

"It's harder than that," I said.

Timby shrugged: have it your way.

Joe was back. He scooted toward me on a stool.

"You, Mrs. Wallace, should inform me the next time you collide with a sculpture and lose consciousness."

"I told him," Timby said with a scrunched-up face.

Joe ripped the paper out of the screen.

My forearm was covered in puncture wounds and torn skin. The whole thing was swollen, red, and gooey with ointment.

"Yowza," I said.

"No broken bones or foreign bodies," Joe said. "We'll give it seventy-two hours to make sure there's no infection." He put on his reading glasses and got in closer. "We might have to close this guy up."

"Joe," I said. "Do you think I'm a mean person?"

"You're not a mean person," he immediately answered, and paused. "You're a mean *nice* person. Big difference."

"See," I said. "I need you for this stuff. You're my Competent Traveler. Don't go all Jesus-y on me."

"Can I go kind of Jesus-y on you?"

"What's Jesus-y?" Timby said.

"Nothing that can't be worked out," Joe said to me. "Genuinely."

"I know that."

We smiled. Our smile.

Joe got up and stuffed the blue paper in the trash can. "Are you aware," he said, "that Thomas Jefferson, the model of reason, called the New Testament 'the most sublime and benevolent code of morals which has ever been offered to man'?"

That's Jesus-y, I mouthed to Timby.

"But," Joe continued, "even Jefferson struggled with its contradictions. So get this. He took a razor blade to the four Gospels and cut out the miracles, mysticism, and other hoo-ha, and pasted the good parts into one coherent story."

"He performed surgery on the Bible," I said.

"There you go!" Joe said.

Then I noticed it, on the wall.

I'd sketched it on our second date. I'd forgotten Joe had saved it. Or that he'd had it framed.

He was still so exotic to me then. I remember the thrill in my stomach. Could he be the one, this serious med student from Buffalo? Brilliant in so many ways, but uncomplicated in his kindness.

And there we were, twenty years after we'd met in an examination room, back in an examination room. Now we were three. My little family.

"I think I can do this," I said.

Joe turned.

"Let's move," I said. "New York, Chicago, Scotland, it doesn't matter."

"We're moving?" Timby asked.

"Even Spokane," I said. "It would be an adventure. A pretty lame adventure. But we *are* old."

"Mom and I need to discuss it," Joe said to Timby.

"Nothing's keeping me in Seattle," I said. "I can draw and do damage anywhere."

"I want to move to Scotland!" Timby said.

"You're full of surprises," Joe said to me.

"I can see the wisdom in what you were saying." I paused to think about it. "If you truly believed you had a benevolent bus driver, and you were certain he was taking you somewhere good, you could just settle in and appreciate the ride."

"You make me sound a little like Yo-Yo," Joe said. "But I'll take it."

First it was my eyes going wide; then it was Timby, gasping.

"Oh, Mom!"

Joe walked across the vast empty parking lot. A moonless night, the only sound the waves lapping in Elliott Bay. The slimmest light blue line traced the top of the Olympic Mountains across the black sound; the sun would set in seconds on the other side.

He stopped and waited. What a striking and chancy thing to witness, a mountain range being absorbed into the dark night sky.

Then Joe saw him, just outside a pool of orange light, sitting politely.

"That's a good boy," Joe said.

Yo-Yo, still tied to the cart rack, swept his tail across the asphalt. Seeing a familiar face, he stood up and wiggled his little behind. As Joe got closer, Yo-Yo pranced and reared. He was always delighted but never surprised that someone had come.

With my good hand, I moved aside the stacks of art books. The hardwood floor was so smooth, the towers glided without toppling. Behind them, a narrow and impractical closet, chockablock like the rest of my tiny workspace. I dug through the crazy quilt of crap. A carton of linen drawing pads I thought I liked but then didn't. That meditation cushion, dusty and sun-bleached. A tangle of phone wire and ancient printer cables. A cache of Sears Wish Books (that's where they were!), forty years' worth, painstakingly collected for reference. A white leather case with Joe's mother's silver. Flashlights from Super Bowl XLVIII. Coconut water from forever ago. Tucked in the way back, the crumpled Neiman Marcus bag.

The Flood Girls.

I set the leather book on my drawing board and turned on the light. The endpaper split when I opened the cover.

Mom and Matty. Every drawing of her looks like a different person. All I had to work off of was my fading, shifting memory. Ivy, my intention was for her to glow. I captured it best in the one with Parsley. The background on the second page: That was from an actual book of nursery tales. Those crayon scribbles done by Ivy's hand. The pillows on the rocking chair, embroidered by Mom, thrown away by the grieving, vengeful nine-year-old me. The guy who wrote the screenplay for *King Kong,* he and his wife used to have us over to watch the Broncos. Matty's chicken scratches. When people die, their handwriting dies too. You don't think about that.

*

I didn't plan not to tell Timby about Ivy. When he was two, I was suffering through a particularly rough stretch of sleepless nights, emotions churned by another new shrink (this one Jungian, this one no help either). Joe and I were in Meridian Park, pushing Timby on a swing. I asked Joe if he hated Ivy and Bucky. He said, "That would make as much sense as hating a rattlesnake. You don't hate rattlesnakes; you avoid them."

When Joe declared on Highway 82 in Aspen that he was done with Ivy, he meant it. I honestly doubt if he's thought about her more than a handful of times since that day. One thing I will say against Joe: He expects me to do the same. Joe can be done with Ivy. I will never be done with Ivy. I don't want to be done with Ivy. She's my sister.

The Aspen map! It took me a month to draw that damned thing. We used to love Richard Scarry and the Sunday *Family Circus*. For our birthdays, Matty would create treasure hunts. These were the only times he allowed us inside the lady's big house. (The rest of the year, he pasted strips of S&H Green Stamps across the front and back doors. He told us he'd written down the serial numbers so we couldn't sneak in.) Those birthday treasure hunts when Ivy and I could finally see the inside: wonders upon wonders.

And the bear. That's a good bear.

"Mom!" Timby called. "Come here!"

I closed the scrapbook. And there it sat amid my jumble. Beautiful, every page of it, drawn by a person I used to be. *The Flood Girls*. Jinxed no more.

Timby was at the mirror on his step stool waiting for me with his toothbrush. If I'd ever had an excuse to skip our routine, it was then. But Timby and I had rarely missed a night standing shoulder to shoulder.

"Look at this!" he said, holding open an *Archie Double Digest*.

I didn't know what I was supposed to be looking at.

"The last line!" Timby said impatiently.

In the panel, Archie and Jughead had just been busted by Mr. Weatherbee for something. Archie turns to Jughead and says, "Grab a rake."

"That's the first time in *Archie* history it doesn't end with an exclamation point!" he said.

My little son. What a smarty. What a sweetie.

"Always ahead of me, you are."

With my good hand, I held out my toothbrush. "Hit me with some of that." Timby squeezed paste on it.

We began brushing.

After a moment, I stopped.

I lowered my toothbrush. I turned to Timby.

"I have a sister," I said. "Her name is Ivy. She's four years younger than I am and she lives in New Orleans with her husband and two children. That means you have an aunt and an uncle and two cousins you've never met."

Timby lowered his hand, leaving his brush sticking out of his foamy mouth. He studied me in the mirror.

Now the hard part.

"Even though they don't know us," I said, "they don't like us."

Timby pulled out his toothbrush, spit into the sink, and looked up.

"They know *you*," he said. "But they don't know *me*."

Today will be different. Today I will be present. Today, anyone I speak to, I will look them in the eye and listen deeply to what they're saying. Today I'll wear a dress. Today I'll play a board game with Timby. I'll initiate sex with Joe. I won't swear. I won't talk about money. Today there will be an ease about me. My face will be relaxed, its resting place a smile. Today I will keep an open mind. Today I won't eat sugar. I'll start to memorize "One Art." Today I'll try to score Timby and me tickets to the Pope. I'll ask around about Scotland. I'll clean out my car. Today I will be my best self, the person I'm capable of being. Today will be different.

Acknowledgments

Thank you…

Anna Stein, Judith Clain, Nicole Dewey

Barbara Heller, Holly Goldberg Sloan, Carol Cassella, Courtney Hodell, Katherine Stirling

Eric Anderson, Daniel Clowes, Patrick Semple

Reagan Arthur, Michael Pietsch, Craig Young, Lisa Erickson, Terry Adams, Amanda Brower, Karen Torres, Keith Hayes, Mario Pulice, Julie Ertl, Andy LeCount, Tracy Roe, Karen Landry, Jayne Yaffe Kemp, Lauren Passell

Arzu Tahsin

Clare Alexander, Mary Marge Locker, Claire Nozieres, Roxane Edouard

Ed Skoog, Kevin Auld, Nicholas Vesey, Phil Stutz, Tim Davis, Kenny Coble

Howard Sanders, Jason Richman, Larry Salz

Joyce Semple, Lorenzo Semple Jr., Johanna Herwitz, Lorenzo Semple III

Peeper Meyer

These pages begin and end with George Meyer, as do I.